A BRIDE FOR GIL

Also by Dusty Richards

A BRIDE FOR GIL

FOR

DUSTY RICHARDS

GALWAY PRESS

AN IMPRINT OF

OGHMA CREATIVE MEDIA

ISBN: 978-1-63373-045-8

Interior Design by Casey W. Cowan
Editing by Gil Miller

Galway Press
Oghma Creative Media
Fayetteville, Arkansas
www.oghmacreative.com

CHAPTER 1

Working cattle with the crew, TXY Ranch foreman Hank Thorpe had a heart attack, fell off his favorite horse, King, and died. I was the jinglebob boss, and we were all set to start spring roundup when, without a word, holding his chest, Hank spilled off his saddle and expired on his back in the dust. Nothing we could do. So all parties agreed we'd put the roundup off for two weeks, and bury him with the respect he deserved.

Two weeks later, Old Man Grimes's black driver, Moses, drove his boss up in a buckboard to our cow camp set up there where all the different outfits were gathered to begin the big annual event. Earl Grimes was in his eighties, a dried up old man, real lame with arthritis. But his blue eyes still could glare down any tough younger man.

"Shame about ole Hank. You're the man in charge, Slatter. I'll pay you his wages. How's things going here?"

"Smooth, but we'll miss him." Grimes could have done this

back at Hank's funeral. He was making a show of it. Power and authority was a game to him.

The old man looked off at the Worthing Mountains. "Yeah, I will, too. But you've got the boots for the job. Pick a guy to take your place. You know these hands better than I do these days. If you don't pick a good one, it'll be your ass gets chewed on, not his if he ain't any account."

"I understand."

Grimes nodded. "This ain't your first job. Gil, I'll see you in ten days or two weeks at the house when the roundup's over. Take care of yourself. Remember you ain't day labor any more. You're the boss. Moses, get my sore bones back to the house."

"Yes, sah." The black man took up his reins and nodded at me, then drove off smartly.

"Gil? Did you get the job?" Clarence, a long drink from Waco, asked me while I watched Grimes's dust and reflected on my new position.

"Did you want the job?" Clarence was an experienced cowboy, and a good man, too.

"Hell, no."

"It may be vacated shortly."

Clarence shook his head in disbelief. "Naw, you'll be all right at it."

"We'll see." I wished I had his full confidence, but I didn't at the moment.

Over the next two weeks or so, we somehow got through roundup without many hitches. Really it had been the usual branding business—bull calves got castrated and their ears notched and hides branded. So were the new heifers—except getting castrated. The various area ranch reps agreed about the calf's momma so the calf wore the right brand. There were sharp words at times, but usually everyone went back to his own camp in the evening and forgot it. Two days of rain was good for the grass and helped fill our tanks, but made us stay out there that much longer to finish up.

We closed up our things, and my camp cook, Norman, and his kid helper, Fuzzy, headed back for the ranch with the chuck wagon. The horse wrangler, a breed teenager named Keeper, took the remuda back. The rest of the crew went into Dog Springs on a two-day holiday to get entertained at Cassie's Whore House, drunk at The Tiger Saloon, and whatever else they wanted to do. I'd paid them the night before—ten bucks a man advance on his thirty-dollar wages for the month. That was a ranch tradition after their long hours and a big job well done.

"If you get the damn clap and can't work, I'll dock you two bucks a day."

They weren't listening to me. I went and found Lex, the easy-riding gray gelding, mounted up, and headed for Thorpe's. He owned a small place east of town. I'd talked some to his daughter at his funeral. Kate was in her early twenties, unmarried. She'd privately asked if I'd come by later and help her with some things. A big girl, she wasn't any beauty queen, but she had pretty, brown, shoulder-length hair. Her eyes were too small, and her mouth looked the same—too small. She never acted coy nor invited a man's attention. In fact, she acted tired about all the time, and I never saw her dance or even take a cowboy's arm at any occasion.

I knew it would be late in the day by the time I reached her small outfit, but I had my bedroll from the wagon behind the cantle just in case. I dropped off the last ridge in the twilight. There was a light on in the house. Good. She hadn't gone to bed.

When I reined up, she stood in the lighted doorway, half of her exposed, when she called out, "That you, Gil?"

"It's me. I'll put Lex in the corral, and I have a bed roll."

"I bet you ain't ate, have ya?"

"No, I rode right over here when we got done with the roundup today."

"I'll make some pancakes. They're quick as anything I can think of to fix. That all right?"

"Sure. Fine."

"You need a light out there?"

"No, I can see all right. Be there in a short while."

"There'll be water on the porch to wash up. Okay?"

"Thanks, Kate."

I unloaded Lex and turned him in the lot. He went off snorting his nose as he headed for the water tank, and rolled in the dirt to stop the itching in his back. I made for the porch to wash up. Hell, if I only knew what she wanted of me. Her father's death and all—she might be confused about some business decision.

From the open front door I could see her form in the kitchen's light. She wore a long blue shifty dress with flowers on it. Must have been a nightdress. I'd never saw her in anything like that before. Her ample body moved under the silken material, exposing her shape. She worked over the stovetop to pour her batter out to make pancakes in two skillets at a time. I washed my hands and face, dried them, and cleared my throat to signal I was coming in.

She turned and nodded. "I was getting ready for bed. I didn't think you'd come tonight."

"I'm sorry. I know all this has been hard on you." I hung my hat and gun belt on a wall hook.

"It won't make any difference. I'm a grown woman. He wouldn't listen to Doc Hardin. Doc told him his heart was failing. But he wasn't going to die in a rocking chair. He made his own decision about that."

"What did you need from me?"

She poured me some fresh smelling hot coffee. Pot in hand, she chewed on her lower lip and looked upset standing there.

"When dad was alive, I'da never done this, but he ain't here. I have wanted for a few years to ask you this. I know I ain't no princess-looking girl, and you can tell me flat out no. But I—I want to be your woman."

She put the coffee pot back on the stove and came right back to stand there. My pancakes were stacked on the plate before me.

Hell, why did she ask me that? "Kate, I'm ten years older'n you are."

"That ain't any excuse." She put her hands flat on the table and stood face to face with me. "Hell, old man Grimes married a kid ten years ago. Forget the age. I don't care if you don't marry me in a church. I'll be your common-law wife if you'll have me. I own this place. It ain't much, but you can run some stock. Dad did."

She moved a small pitcher of syrup beside the plate for me. "You eat now. I know you're shocked. It sure wasn't easy for me to tell you all that. I'm sure not some elegant speaker, but I am a very serious person, and I can help you."

I shook my head to clear it. How did I ever get into this mess? "Kate, I ain't looking for a wife."

"Just eat. We can talk more afterwards." She sat down on the end chair close to me.

"You buy that outfit you're wearing for this occasion?" I asked, figuring I was supposed to be seeing what I'd saw.

"No, I made it myself, though, for this. . . time. I make all my own clothes, and I made all of dad's shirts. Do you like it?"

I took a bite of her rich pancakes and nodded as I chewed. Saliva was running in my mouth. They were damn good. "I thought it was an expensive outfit you'd bought."

"I don't look like a—a dove in it, do I?"

"No. Nothing like that, Kate. I guess I'd call it real cute." I looked over at her sitting there. Her thick, full hair shone in the lamplight as she twisted a handful of it from beside her face.

"I ain't crazy, Gil. I need to survive. This place is paid for, but I need to eat and breathe. That will take some money. Not a lot, but I have no skills to make any."

"You can really sew. I recall your daddy's fine shirts you made him."

Chewing on her full lower lip, she nodded in agreement. "You got an old one and like the way it fits, leave it here. I can make you one just like it."

"I ain't a man would lie to you if you and I—well, I mean. Hell, I ain't never been asked to decide anything like this."

"Eat."

She slipped closer on the chair beside me. "I won't ever nag you. I promise. You tell me what you want, and if I can do it, I'll deliver it to you."

The pancakes were sure good tasting. The knot in my guts over her wants was the only thing for me to overcome. Was she a virgin? I know she mentioned—no, I imagined she said so. Ah, who in the hell cared about that, anyway?

I sipped the tongue-pleasing coffee. This wasn't a bad place—damn sure nice kept.

"You ever been with a man?" I up and asked her.

"You mean in bed?"

I felt like a fool for asking her that. "Yeah."

"Gil, I have never kissed any man. Is that good enough?"

"Stand up." She obeyed me.

Then I stood up from the chair and stepped over to her. I squeezed her in my arms. She was two arms' full of body to hug. "Stop chewing on your lip."

"I can't. I'm trembling inside. I always said to myself—if he'd ever held me, I'd never let him go. I ain't half as brave as I figured I would be, am I?"

"Hell girl, don't ask me. I am getting excited just holding you."

She slapped my shoulder. "You're the leader in this deal."

I bent over and kissed her hard on the mouth. Then I believed her. She'd damn sure never been kissed before. But she got lots of the notion on how to do that the longer we were kissing.

At last out of wind, she huffed for her breath, but I kept her standing there in my arms like she belonged to me. "Was that like you imagined it would be?"

"I'm floating. Is that all right?"

I squeezed her against me. "Yes, that's right."

Her arms wrapped around me and she laid her cheek on my shoulder. "You still testing me?"

"Yes, why?"

She nuzzled my vest. "I have never been this intimate with another human being in my entire life. My mother died when I was ten. I don't recall her ever. . . ever hugging or kissing me. I guess she never did."

Her words caused a knot behind my tongue I couldn't swallow. I knew Hank had never hugged her, either. I held her tight. "If you ever have children, Kate, you hug and kiss them every day for them being on this earth."

"I promise. I promise."

"I need to go see the old man in the morning. Hell knows what he needs. But you'll have to wake me before sunup and kick my ass out."

"He made you foreman?"

"Oh, yes."

"I expected that to happen."

"No matter—I need to be over there in the morning."

"I have an alarm clock." She was laughing. Sounded more nervous like than whole-hearted fun, but I knew it was the tension inside her doing that to her. "Gil Slatter, I won't ever kick you anywhere."

"I mean I have to be there."

"I understand. I won't let you be late."

I looked down at her. "Do you have anything on under this dress?"

She blushed in the flickering lamplight. "Do I need some more on?"

"Lord, no. Just curious. There must be twenty buttons to undo."

"I can—"

I caught and squeezed her hands. "No, you said you were a present to me."

She nodded, appearing shaken. "I did. I. . . am."

I kissed her. This time she was in on it, and I have to admit it was thrilling. Opening the buttons one at a time soon exposed the tops of her full breasts. She looked away a little red-faced.

"Should I stop?"

Her forehead fell to my chest, and she whispered, "No, I want you to want me. But I am getting weak-kneed thinking that when you finally see me naked, you'll run away."

I raised her chin and kissed her on the mouth. "Am I acting like a guy that's going to run away when I see all of you?"

"No."

"Good. I want tonight to be our glorious honeymoon, not some cheap un-thought-out deal for pleasure."

Tears ran down her cheeks. "You're going to do it. Aren't you?"

"I accepted your terms. Is that all right?"

"Oh, Gil, if you knew how I have prayed—how many ways—how many times. I won't say another word." She took the kerchief from me, mopped her face, and snuffed her nose. "But you better hurry. I may faint."

I got busy unbuttoning the dress and swept it off her round shoulders, exposing her snowy body. She looked like a large bowl of home-churned ice cream to me in the lamp light. I shed my vest. With her shaky fingers, she undid my shirt buttons while I toed off my boots. Then acting without restraint, she kissed my chest, and hugged me to her large breasts.

I shed my britches. She put them on a chair and came right back. We hugged and kissed.

"Let's use your bed."

"Yes," She hugged my waist like she feared I'd leave her, and we stepped over to the steel poster bed.

I stopped her after she swept back the bedcover. "If you want off the train, here is the depot. You need to stop this, you tell me right now."

"Don't stop." Her lashes wet, she shook her head again to reinforce her answer. "I don't want off. I'm excited, Gil. I swear I never dreamed this far. Never thought you'd accept my deal."

"It gets real serious from here on."

"Let's go." She climbed on the bed and dropped on her side. The ropes under her protested, and I moved to join her.

"Where do I need to be here?" she asked.

"Center of the bed to start."

She scooted over there. "What next?"

"I'll kiss you until you surrender."

She swallowed. I could read her fear and pent up excitement when I fed on her firm breasts. Her nipples soon pointed out, and she was halfway to being damn shaken. I was too. I didn't know that much about women, my wham-bang deals with whores and putas were all quick and over. All I wanted from those women was some male relief, and they gave it. This was a lot more permanent, so I needed to take my time and enjoy it as well as her, too.

"Relax. If it hurts it will only be for a second."

Man, she sure felt good to be joined to. Her hair was in her face, and she tossed it around, moaning softly. Wow, she was really going to be fun to make love to. She might never have expected doing this—I sure never had even imagined making love to her would be this great, or I'd been more attentive to her years ago.

We were floating in the air. It wouldn't be half bad to have a wife to treat me like this every time I came home. And by damn, I'd teach her how to dance. I'd danced since I was a little kid, and if she could make love like this she could dance. Man-oh-man, we went on and on forever. I was having the most fun in my entire life, and she was the center of my attention. At last two bolts of lightning struck me. She fainted.

"You all right?"

She pulled me down and kissed me. "I fainted. Oh, God, I never fainted in my whole life before tonight. If this is our life ahead, I love it. You're so neat, so gentle. Can I scream?'

"Hell down here, you can scream all you want."

I was up on my knees, and she cupped her mouth. "Yee-hoo!"

By then I was laughing so hard I could cry.

"Let me up. This business is messy on my end of it," she said. I moved so she could roll over and get off the bed, but not before she puckered up and leaned over to kiss me.

"I won't leave you long," she promised.

Standing on the round rag rug on the floor, I was tired, drained out. But I also felt amazed how neat she turned out to be as a lover. I'd figured this mating business was going to be charity work on my part, but instead it turned out to be neater than a dream. Dad would have said, "Ya gotcha a round one, boy."

My mom was skinny as a rail, and her breasts went plumb flat after ten kids suckled on them. He'd courted her in Arkansas and married her at fourteen. She had Israel before she was fifteen. They were coming to Texas by wagon and he was born before they ever got to Texarkana. Then she lost a girl. I was born around Tyler the following year. Tough life, but we had food. Shot lots of game. Gardened, kept a cow. Broke mustangs for work horses and saddle horses. Raised some corn, some cotton. Paw said it was better farming ground than the hills they left, Maw said at least at night up there it got cool—never did that at night in Texas in the summer time.

War came, we went to war. Five of us boys—Ulysses was fourteen. He was the youngest of us. They killed him first. Israel and me were the only two came home after the war. Craig and Hiram, we never heard how they died. Neighbor boys told us they were lost at the end while with them. They were buried somewhere in the Mississippi mud.

Israel married his sweetheart, Ginger Brown, and they moved to Fort Worth. I lost track of him. Tried a time or two to find him, but I guess he'd moved on. Paw died first, and I was up in Kansas with a big herd and found out in a letter when I got to Abilene. Maw only lasted a year more. My sisters all were married and gone. So I had no family roots back there. But at last clear out here in west Texas I'd found me a woman. The naked one who came right back and had cleaned herself all up for me.

"What's next?" she asked. And I thought she was the lazy one—she had more perk than I did.

But hugging her some standing there, I got anxious, too. So we did it again. She was kissing me like she'd been doing that since she was born.

We finally fell asleep, and by damn her alarm had me up before five. Both of us were sitting up naked in bed. Hell with it. We had time for another round.

After that I shaved while she made us more pancakes and coffee. Her busy cooking, I could rub her backside and squeeze it before I kissed her on the neck. That was kind of nice. Poor girl had never been paid any attention. She soaked it all in. I slipped up behind her, squeezed her, and she sucked in her breath. Then I kissed her some on the smooth skin of her neck, and she wiggled back against me.

We were plumb obsessed with each other.

Later she put on her fancy nightdress and ate with me. After our meal, she went with me to the corral, and I saddled the gray.

"You know when you will be back?" she asked.

I dug out some money. "You got a store bill?"

"No, and I still have money."

"Buy some material. And when you get time, this shirt is my size." I got it out of my saddlebags for her. Kinda anxious to have me a nice shirt to wear 'cause she made such good ones.

She took it and fit it on my back. Tested the sleeve length and nodded.

"Here's money for the material." I made her take it. "I'll back Saturday evening unless we have trouble. And I can stay through Sunday. I don't need that shirt like right now. You've got chores enough to do around here."

"I'll be here, Gil. Waiting for you."

"Mrs. Slatter, I'll be back looking for you quick as I can. I never had a woman, so if I get out of hand, blame my ignorance and be patient with me. Is that all right, Mrs. Slatter?"

"Oh, gawdamn you! Gil Slatter that is the nicest thing anyone ever said to me."

I kissed her and left her crying. Damn that woman, anyway.

CHAPTER 2

The old man was coughing hard when I went across the porch to the front door of the big house. He was back in the building somewhere, but I could hear him barking good. His black cook, Mandy, came to the door.

"Mr. Grimes is expecting you, Mr. Slatter. Come in, sir."

"Call me Gil. Being foreman don't mean nothing to you and me, Mandy."

"He calls you Mr. Slatter since he came home."

"I'm still Gil."

"He's really coughing this morning. I worry a lot about him." She lowered her voice. "Long as he's alive, I's got me a job, but ain't no telling when he dies what that bitch of a wife of his will be like to please."

"I bet you'll please her."

"No way. No way."

"She here?"

"Naw, she's in Dallas or San Antonio. She can stay there long as she wants."

I found the old man sitting up in his nightclothes, swallowed by the large bed and all the white cotton sheets and pillows. His snowy hair looked thin on top of the tight, purple-veined skin on his head. His bushy white eyebrows were untrimmed.

A scowl matched his words. "What took you so damn long?"

"It rained two days."

"I expected you back here last night."

"What broke down?"

He said, "A windmill."

"You miss a bath over it?"

"Who did you choose to be your second in command?" he asked.

"I haven't. Didn't need one so far. I ain't made my mind up. I will."

"You want to fire any of them?"

"Not today."

"You need to get your bluff in on them and quick."

"I don't use bluff. It ain't my style. I don't chew out men to show I'm boss, but if they cross me, they will learn my patience is on a short fuse."

"What are you going to do next?"

"Move some bulls. Three of them stay around that Reynolds Creek Ford. I'm sending them in three directions and replacing them with that older shorthorn bull they call Scotland who's up on the flats. I have locations picked for those three. They aren't getting cows bred. Taking turns on them that are easy to catch around there. That's what you have them for, right? To breed cows?"

Grimes almost smiled.

"Going to cut out all those dry cows that don't have calves, and cull them if we can't bump calves in them."

"How many are there?"

"Several. We haven't cut but some old canners out the last few years. Thorpe said they'd calve, leave them. Well, they ain't going to do nothing but eat our grass."

He nodded. No more grumpy comments, so I knew I had his attention.

"There's a young bull I saw out in the Worthings that has a broken toe. I'll replace him and bring him down here in a bull wagon and see if we can shoe him and save him."

"Shoe an ox, huh?"

"I've seen it work."

Grimes shook his head as if amused. "You ever tell Old Man Thorpe this?"

"No. He wasn't interested."

"I bet he wasn't. You were crowding him, you know that?"

"I worked for him. I never applied for his job. He was just insecure."

"Maybe he was."

"He knew his heart was weak. He ever tell you that?"

"No. What did he know?"

"His daughter Kate said the doc told him twice that his heart was failing him. She said he had no aim to die in a rocking chair."

"I can understand that. How well do you know her?"

"Well enough. Now I have this job, I'm going to marry her."

"Big wedding?"

"She and I will have something simple. No big deal."

He sat there looking a little less tired, not near as stern than he had been in the times past with me.

"I like your ideas. Now can you do them?"

"I can. We need two dozen new horses. Thorpe never spent any money on them, but we're riding too many crow baits. I can get some from the Comanche up in the Indian Territory. Ten bucks a head. Ranch hands can break them."

"I thought the army shot all their horses."

"Not all of them, and they always need money."

"Why not buy three dozen? You can break them, and the overage could make us some money." Grimes looked hard at me for an answer.

"Sure, I can buy that many. I may take a honeymoon and go buy them. Go up there and hire some boys to drive them back. They'd be cheaper than some of our men going up there. "

"Hell, you don't have a man to take your place—yet."

"I will before I leave."

Grimes squeezed his white whisker-grizzled jaw. "She's a serious woman, ain't she?"

"Yes. She won't talk your leg off, either."

"That's a gawdamn good blessing in a woman. Gil Slatter, I'm proud you're the man. I like your ideas. You get back from the Territory, you can take her with you to Fort Worth and find us a market for the big steers this fall. But get the jinglebob man in place first."

"I'll do that. Where's the windmill squealing at?"

Grimes shook his head to dismiss it as nothing. "I can recall having to go by to see a woman, too. Good luck with that part."

"Yes, sir." I left him coughing. One thing I knew, if the devil was going to take that ornery old man, it would be him kicking and squalling all the way to hell. Me telling him about Kate had surprised him, and he'd softened up too with us talking.

I'd had Clarence Logan on my mind since before he asked me about my having the foreman job. I left the big house and found him in the blacksmith shop. He was handy at that work. We were alone in the shadowy building that reeked of burning coal in his forge. Sweaty faced, he sliced the beads off his forehead with his finger and flung them aside.

"Anything wrong?" he asked.

"Let's get out of here into the air outside."

We stepped out under the shade of the cottonwood. "You want ten more a month?"

"You offering me the jinglebob job?" He threw a hard glance at the distant house like he wanted to know what Grimes thought of it.

"Yes. You want to take it?"

"I'd be fool not to, wouldn't I?"

"No. That's your decision. I think you can handle men and get the job done."

"I guess that's how you get to be a foreman, huh? You ain't thinking about dying, are ya?"

"Hell no." I clapped him on the shoulder. "There's more to this story. Kate Thorpe and I are getting married. I have to go buy some horses up in the Nation, and then go to Fort Worth and find a market for our steers."

"Your new wife going along?"

I nodded.

He made a pained face. "I'd never figured she was your type."

I chuckled, amused at his assumption. "What did you figure was my type?"

"The old man's wife."

His words sobered me. "No, I never gave her anything but a hard look. A man like me could never satisfy someone fancy as her. You can have her."

"I'm lucky to keep some ugly dove from complaining about me being in bed with her as it is. I sure couldn't handle that one. Whew."

"Anyway, you and a couple of boys grease that number two buckboard and match me up a good team. I'll take Lex along. Need some mess stuff, food for a couple of weeks, and a water barrel. Oh, you know. What do you say about the job?"

He shoved out his calloused hand. "I'll be proud to be your man."

We shook.

"I'm going back to the house. You ring the bell and call the hands in. We'll have a powwow with the men down there by the cook shack."

"What will he say?"

"That it will be my ass if you screw up."

Clarence chuckled. "Glad it will be yours and not mine."

"You won't have one left. I ain't Thorpe, and I do things different. Teach you a smithy or find one for this work. You'll have enough to do."

Headed back to the house, I heard him pealing the bell. I knocked. Mandy told me to come in. "He's eating in the kitchen."

"Thanks."

Grimes looked up with a loaded spoon full of soup. "Yes?"

"You know Clarence Logan?"

"Tall thin guy?"

"That's him."

"He's the guy that's so good at blacksmithing?" Grimes slurped his soup.

"Yes, and I told him he needed to hire or teach someone how to do that."

"That's reasonable. When will the honeymoon start?"

"Day after tomorrow."

Grimes had finished his spoon and used it like a club to cut the air with. "Don't you know a woman is supposed to set the wedding day?"

"It won't bother her none."

"You gathering the crew now to tell them?"

"Yes, I plan to leave Thursday to go get those horses."

"You want a bank draft or cash to buy them?"

"Indians won't take a check."

"I'll have it in silver and your expense money."

"Thank you. Clarence can handle things. I better go give her the plans."

"Sure, do that. You have your man. Gil, I like your plans. You've been looking at things like a boss. Tell her I wish you two to have the best life together."

"I'll do that, sir. She's different than most women. But she suits me."

"You be careful too up there," Mandy said. "All of us need you back here."

"I'll do that for you, Mandy."

"I's sure hope you do."

"See, you even have my housekeeper concerned. Go talk to those men, and then see about your bride. You may have your first argument out of wedlock." Grimes chuckled and went for more soup.

"Clarence is fixing the number two buckboard today for us to take."

Grimes took another mouthful of soup. He nodded in approval. Swallowed and told me, "Those boys will be waiting."

"I can handle that."

Grimes agreed and settled in to eat his lunch of soup with soda crackers.

I left the house, prepared for my first speech as their foreman, and the introduction of my man, Clarence, as the man in charge when I was gone. I could do that. It was her I was hurrying to get back to. Would it always be like that, me wanting to get back to her? That might be nice.

CHAPTER 3

I loped Lex most of the way back to Kate's place. She ran from the garden to see who was coming at that speed. When she saw it was me, her face looked afraid like something was wrong.

I brought Lex to a sliding stop. Then I bailed out of the saddle, threw my arms around her, lifted her off her feet, and swung her around.

"Silly, you're going to break your back throwing me around." She was trying to get me to put her down.

"Kiss me, damn it."

"Oh yeah, I said I'd do anything you asked me to do."

She really kissed me, and I let her slip back onto her feet. We were still kissing when she was settled. Oh I couldn't get enough of her mouth or she of mine.

"We're taking a honeymoon going to Fort Sill Thursday. I need to buy some horses for the ranch."

Disbelief was written on her face. She blinked her brown-green eyes at me. "You mean. . . we're having a real honey-moon?"

"Why, you gave me lots of leeway in this deal. Wife? Common-law one? Either one needs a honeymoon, don't they?"

"Oh yes. What was last night?" Her stomach pressed against my gun belt buckle, and her thin dress was wet with her sweat—no doubt she'd been busy working hard.

"Hell that was a trial run—" Then I kissed her hard and came up for air. "We'll have near two weeks to camp out by ourselves. If you can stand being with me that long."

"Oh, I never dreamed—"

"I love you, woman. There's so much you never dreamed about that I can show you. Have you ever been to Fort Worth?"

Her face looked pale. "No, why?"

"We'll need to go in there next and sell some cattle."

She sagged in my arms. "Are you serious?"

"Hey, bet you never dreamed of that, either."

She shook her head. "My brain is whirling. What's next?"

"I'll catch Lex and put him up."

"I'll go, too. I really did not think I'd ever be this bound to another person. I am tied to you, and I need to be all the time."

"The old man said a funny thing. The wedding day was the bride's choice. Not mine. I said she'd take me any day. I'm so dumb, what did he mean?"

"Oh, he's talking about the curse of Eve."

"What in the hell is that?"

"You had sisters. Didn't they bleed once a month?"

"Yeah, sure." My memory came back about that fuss.

"Well, a woman usually knows when that will happen. She wouldn't want it to happen on her wedding day. That's why, huh?"

"You are probably right. We won't hit it tomorrow, will we?"

"No. Not for a week I hope to hell."

"Good." I hugged her. There was so much to learn about having a wife—I might never get it all.

"Hey, I'm sorry, Gil. I catch myself swearing all the time around you. Tap me on the lip when I do that. I lived out here all alone and picked up that habit when I was disgusted. I'll be twenty-one in six months. Your momma got married at what age?"

"Fourteen."

"See, here I am twenty-one. That might be why I swear. But I will bite my tongue and not swear anymore—but if I do, will you remind me?"

"Kate, I am so glad to have you. It wasn't time wasted, and we ain't kids anymore, either. It don't help you much to have a mate like me who cusses."

She smiled up at me while we headed for the house holding hands. "Don't you worry. I'm just proud to be listening to you anytime."

She held a fist to her bust line. "It gets me right here hearing you talking to me. Thorpe never really talked to me. He'd say something I better listen, but he said it off-handed. Like, 'Fix the water tank.'"

At the door, I swept her up and kissed her. It took her breath away. Neat deal, my wife not being spoken to until I came along. Damn, she'd missed a lot of simple human contact. Shame about that, but now we had each other, and we could make that up.

"I'll fix lunch," she said. "It will take a few minutes. I wasn't expecting you. What did Grimes know?"

"Not much. Did Thorpe tell you much about him when he came home?"

"Oh, you mean that old s.o.b.? That's what he called him. He'd come home so mad he'd be grinding his teeth."

"I cut his bitching off this morning. He said he expected me to be there the day before. I simply asked him what windmill was squeaking."

"Oh, no." She suppressed her amusement to listen.

"He got over his bitching."

"I think you're going to make a helluva foreman for him." She ran her calloused palm up the side of my face, and then gently slapped me.

"You didn't get those calluses sitting around, did you?"

She looked at her palm and scowled. "I guess they're not a nice woman's hands."

"The hell they aren't. I love them."

"Good. I'll make lunch with them."

I put up my hat and gun belt on a wall peg, then took a chair at the table. "It will be kind of rough camping out going to Fort Sill."

"I'm not some little girl. I'll be fine."

"Well. I thought—"

"Gil, don't baby me. I am a big ole girl. I can outshoot most men. And I'm not some little social bee. When the going gets tough, I'll be tougher, too."

"I know. I just don't want you to get hurt."

"I appreciate that. I want you to think Kate is with me, and she's tough as anyone."

I chuckled. "I'm not laughing at you. I want you with me."

"Good." She rolled out her dough, then she used a floured whiskey jigger to cut biscuits out.

"Have you ever danced?"

She drew her face up and looked hard at me. "When I got some ants in my pants one day."

Damn she was a mess. Ants. "I mean danced with a boy?"

"No. Who'd ever dance with me?"

"Your husband."

She put her flour-dusted hand to her face and mouth. Then she held up her hand to ask for a moment. After her pause she said, "I told you, I'd do whatever you asked of me.

I was running off at the mouth there. I'm sorry, but remember you are my one and only social contact. If you want to try and teach me, yes, I'll learn how to dance." She held her head high. "You won't regret it, either."

"You know what?"

"I have no da—idea."

"We're going to have lots of fun together."

"Let me tell you what is so neat."

"What is that?"

"Well, first you listen to me. I can tell you what is on my mind, and you don't scoff at me. And I feel like the two of us are living in a bubble." She made a circle with her floury hands before she went and washed them.

"Yes, all that and more in only twenty-four hours."

She looked down, shaking her head as she dried her hands. "I thought this morning when I woke up that we'd already been together for a lifetime."

I stood up and hugged her. "It has been, darling. It really has."

The next morning Judge Harold Beamer married us in his office. His secretary was the witness. Then we rode out to the ranch, and I reintroduced her to Grimes and his house crew. Mandy hugged her and cried. Grimes beamed like he was her father and gave me the trip and horse money. Then we rode down to the cook shack, and I introduced her to Clarence, Norman, Fuzzy, and Keeper.

Clarence told us to wait and went to the bunkhouse. He came back with a gold ring and tried to hand it to me. "I'll never use this ring. My mother wore it."

"Hell, I can't take it."

Clarence made a face. "It ain't for you, silly. Try it on her."

He handed her the ring, and like magic the band slipped down her finger. "Clarence, may I kiss you?" she asked.

"Hell, I don't know."

I gave him a shove. Bashful damn cowboy. "Kiss the bride."

He did and about made me feel jealous. There I discovered I was fast becoming possessive toward her, too.

"You two be careful going up there." Clarence stepped back and shook his head. "I'm jealous as all hell that he got you, Kate."

"Take care of my ranch," I said to him, and herded her to the horses.

"Thanks for the ring, Clarence," she said over her shoulder.

"I have the buckboard loaded," Clarence shouted. "It's all ready. May as well take it home with you."

I reined up Lex at a small distance from him and scowled at her. "I about forgot it."

"My fault," she said under her breath so no one could hear. "I wanted you back in our bed."

"I know. Let's get it and drive it home."

"Fine."

I twisted in the saddle and thanked him.

We found the buckboard all wrapped up in red and white paper. What a mess. It looked set up. They even had the harnessed team there ready to hitch and drive away. Before we took off, I checked the box for what they had loaded for us. Plenty of grub in there. I knew Norman had loaded it for us. After I dropped the lid on the full chuck box and stepped off the wagon bed, I saw Kate was crying.

"Mrs. Slatter. What's wrong now?"

She came over and hung her arms on my shoulder. "They did this for you. That crew really likes you. But I didn't ever dream of having a gold ring. That or you ever really marrying me. You didn't have to do that. I told you—"

My finger on her mouth, I silenced her. "You said you'd be my common-law wife. I didn't intend to do that to you. Can you drive the team?"

"Why of course I can."

I boosted her up on the spring seat. "Don't turn it over."

She undid the reins and nodded. "I promise not to wreck it."

"Good." I watched her start out, then went and got the two saddle horses. Wasn't much that a man could do she couldn't do just as well. I had to short-lope Lex to catch her, and we were home in a few hours.

At our place, she double-checked the box for what they'd loaded for us to eat. I had taken my bedroll off the cantle and handed it to her, so she strapped it on.

"That will work for both of us, won't it?" she asked.

"Wide enough for one deep enough for two. I guess it will work."

Shaking her head and laughing, she frowned at my joke. "I've got to get used to a man picking on me."

"Lots you have to get used to, innocent one."

All of our horses put up quick-like, I caught and kissed her. "Let's take a bath and honeymoon all clean with no scruffy beard."

"How will I bake some bread and goodies to take along?"

"I don't know."

She gave me a shove. "What're you waiting for, standing here?"

"Soap."

"Silly, you saw the sheepherder shower. Get up there and get undressed. I have soap and towels at the house. I'll join you."

"Don't run." I kissed her, and she lifted her hem and ran for it—like I had told her not to do.

The water was not hot, but it was fun washing each other under the spray when I pulled the handle. Exploring is what I called our bath. She told me she'd heat water and shave me at the house. I took her up on it. In no time, two stark naked bodies hurried across the yard with our arms full of clothes, boots, shoes, and a gun. My wife shaved me, and we spent some time on her bed.

Lying on our backs side by side and staring at the underside of the cedar shingle roof, she asked, "Is that first born we've been making going to be Gilmore Junior?"

I shook my head. "I'll be thinking on that one and give you a list."

"You've got plenty of time to choose one."

"What if it's a girl? Do I name her?"

"Sure. What is it going to be?"

"Octavia."

"Why that poor kid would hide out all the time bearing a name like that."

"Yeah, but she'd be her daddy's pet. And have everything she wants."

"Oh."

"You treat me like that. You'll be worse with her."

We rolled together and kissed. I felt damn impressed by her efforts to spoil me. A man could have done a lot worse. And to think she'd set her star on me was fulfilling.

She stayed up half the night baking things anyway. But she still got me up before dawn. We had to stop by and see an old man that was her neighbor. He'd already told her he'd feed her stock and look after our things.

Henny Brown was his name, and he was busy hoeing in his garden. I reined up close—she introduced me.

"Oh, Henny, this big guy is my husband, Gil."

"Good to meet'cha. Where you two going?"

"On our honeymoon."

"I knew that. But where?"

"Fort Sill," I said.

He made a sour face. "Lord, there ain't much to see up there but Injuns' back sides."

She laughed, sat back, and we were off.

We camped the first night in a copse of oaks. That's a ring of post-oak trees that grew up like mushrooms in a circle. That brand of trees themselves never grew that fast. They made sorry lumber and were the worse if you ever tried to use them for logs in a cabin. But I found enough dead wood for the fire and chopped up some more to take along. Farther north and west, fuel except for cow chips would be scarce.

The fire burned down to some orange blue flames licking the air. We sat cross-legged together making small talk and listened to the night insects beginning a chorus. A coyote or two set out on night hunt. Some horses came on the little-traveled road.

"We're having company."

She nodded, then got up and went over to the buckboard. The Winchester was in a scabbard on the dashboard. She returned, and sat back down with it across her lap. Only as a precaution since we were isolated out there.

"Can't tell who's coming," she said.

I agreed. When they drew closer, I rose.

Short of the firelight one of them shouted, "Hello the camp. We're peaceful."

"Light down. We don't have any food left. Sorry."

"We ate—" He noticed Kate and removed his hat with a nod. "Didn't mean to bother you two. How far is it up to the Red River?"

The others set their horses as silhouettes in the night.

"I guess at least a two days' ride north."

"Is there a ferry up there?"

"Use to be. I haven't been up this way in a few years. I'm hoping there is."

"So do I," the unshaven man in his thirties said and turned to go back to his horse. "Oh, thanks ma'am, you too." Then when he reached his horses, he said to the others. "He ain't sure, but thinks so."

They rode off under the stars.

"I think they're outlaws," she said, looking off in the inky night full of crickets chirping.

"Could have been. The Indian Territory is full of them."

"You reckon they might swing back tonight?"

"I'll set up and keep guard."

"Not by yourself. I'll take part of the night. I'm a full partner."

"I'll take watch for a couple of hours, then trade off with you."

"Fair enough. Should we sleep under the buckboard?"

"Behind it."

"You reckon they'll try anything?" She was on her knees to get up and handed me the rifle.

"Desperate men do desperate things. They better not try."

She was standing before me, ready to be kissed. "I love you, Gil. Those men could have been hardened killers, you never wavered a minute. It was simple. They wanted trouble, you had trouble for them."

"Get some sleep. I'll wake you for your turn."

"You better."

I kissed her and sent her to bed. It would be a long night.

Why did I feel they might try something? She felt the same. Worse, why did they have to come by on our honeymoon? Maybe nothing would happen, but I figured we had enough for some two-bit outlaws to consider taking it all. This north end of Texas wasn't a rich place for robbers.

I sat away from the fire, used the front wagon wheel for a chair back, and she had draped a blanket over me. The night was cooling off.

For my part. I hoped if they were coming back, they did it early, and we got it over with. No telling, it simply might be a long creaky night when I could have been snuggled with my wife. Damn their souls.

The Big Dipper finally showed midnight. Time to wake her for a few hours. I could finish the guarding out later. Rifle leaned against the wagon wheel, I straightened up stiff-like and went to wake her.

She was sleeping in her nightdress and woke quickly. "What time is it?"

"About midnight by my calculations. Wake me at two?"

"Three."

"You can read the Big Dipper?"

"I'm Hank Thorpe's daughter. Yes I can."

"Good. I'll sleep till—"

"Three. Give me the six-gun."

I undid the gun harness and handed it to her while stealing a quick kiss. "Wake me if you hear anything."

"No problem. Get some sleep. No wife to sleep with you."

"I ain't taking that too good, either."

She laughed, and I went to catch some sleep. It was only a few minutes I thought since I'd done that, and she was whispering in my ear. "We've got company coming." Her finger silenced me before I could speak. "They are on both sides of us right now."

She slid the rifle in my hands as I moved the covers aside. Then, on my belly, I put the rifle in a position ahead of me, pointed toward the road.

"I'll get the ones back there," she said, indicating behind us.

I agreed. Straining my ears, I heard the shuffle of boot soles. They were close. In the starlight, a figure moved into my sight, and I squeezed off a shot. My victim screamed. Another figure began firing at us, and I cut him down with the next two bullets.

She fired the Colt .45 and then again. Four times, and then the sound of footfalls and a horse or two charging off came to my aching ears. I wasn't certain. One, maybe two got away. No matter, they left us unscathed in a fog of acrid gun smoke. I pulled her to her feet, and we moved to escape the bitter cloud from the smoke. Bent over and coughing, eyes burning, I tried to regain our breath. I glanced over and saw she was doing the same.

I took the Colt from her and stuck it in my waistband.

"It has one more shot in it," she warned me.

"I counted them too. You all right?"

"Shaking inside. And my eyes are burning."

I hugged her shoulder. "You did great."

She nodded. "You think they're dead?"

"We need to be careful. A wounded snake can still bite you."

"There's a small coal oil light in the wagon. It's in a wooden case."

"Good, I'll get it. Keep the rifle handy."

Standing over the open chuck box in the starlight, I found the case and took out the small lamp. To test the fuel I shook it. There was some in the base. Back on the ground I struck a match, raised the globe, and lighted the wick. When I had a light, she joined me.

"Good."

I took the rifle, gave her the light, and we started for the two on the ground, her holding the lamp high enough for me to see the way with the rifle ready in my clammy hands. It wasn't a great light, but beat none at all, and we found them. One was on his back, one on his belly. If they were alive, they made little sign of it. I swept up their pistols and nudged each with my boot toes. Nothing.

"They're dead?"

"I think so. Let's go and see about the one in the west."

Side by side, we cautious-like started back, and I put their weapons on the tail of the buckboard bed. We found the one she shot sprawled in some brush, and when I took his gun away he moaned, "Sons a bitches. . . ."

"Who got away?" I demanded.

"Ray Cline. He'll. . . get'cha."

"He best come in his Sunday suit. I aim to send him to hell on sight."

I grabbed his arm and drug him out of the brush on his back, him screaming and cussing at me the whole way, but I didn't give a damn. He should've known better.

I gave him a sharp kick to the ribs. "Shut up. There's a woman here."

"Fuck her."

He got a harder kick for that and shut up.

"Let's make breakfast," I said to her.

"What will we do with them?"

"Load them belly down over their horses and take them to the next town."

"It may kill that last one."

"I don't care. They'd have shot us, raped you, and cut our throats. I have no concern for him. And my trail will cross with this Ray Cline, and I'll get him too, someday."

She was on her knees, building a fire under her grill-like stove. Using the lamp, she busied herself getting things going in the pre-dawn darkness. I squatted on my boot heels and cleaned the barrel of the .45, then reloaded it. I'd need to do a better job later. For the moment, I wanted it reloaded in case we had more trouble. The cartridge model revolver was the new one and much easier to handle than the older cap and ball models. I slapped on my holster, put it on my waist, and buckled it up.

I squatted down beside her and rubbed her shoulders as she worked. "This has not been a great day in our lives. But I thank you. You are tough as any man I ever had beside me in the war or any other time that I was in a rough place."

Tears running down her cheeks, she raised her head. "I have thanked God for you, and after this morning I thanked Him again. Before the shooting ever started, I saw you shot to death in my mind and knew I had to prevent that."

"You did a super job."

We kissed, and I dried her face with my kerchief. "Kate, no one is going to get us. I promise. The Yankees didn't. Mexican bandits stabbed at it, and two whiskey traders in Kansas tried, but none of them are breathing today."

She turned, and we kissed long and hard. Once we released each other, she made a smile in the fire's light. "We better save the lamp and its fuel. I bet we need it again."

"I'm buying us a bigger one and a can of fuel at the next store we find."

She chuckled. "It really wasn't much light, was it?"

"Naw, but hey, we made it do."

"I'm slow this morning. I'll have it ready soon."

"Hey, this isn't a horse race. I'll go saddle Lex and gather their horses at daylight."

"Fine. You can't rush water boiling."

I didn't need any lamp to find my horse. The animal was grazing. Hobbled, he raised his head at my approach. I put a rope on his neck and undid the hobbles, then led him to the buckboard. A great mount, I hoped to find some more like him up at Fort Sill. After brushing dirt and any sticks off his back, I clapped him on the neck.

I hoped the horses I found up there to buy were as good as Lex. I had no idea about his origin. When I got to the ranch, he was already in the remuda. A hand that used him had quit. I chose him and another bay horse in his string. The bay was a stout horse to rope large stock, but not near as easy to ride long distance as the gray.

I had five others, mostly used horses. Over half of the ranch's using horses were stove up and aged. Even the old man agreed about that.

Thorpe wasn't going to rile the old man about buying more. Like a lot of things, it hadn't been worth it to him to defend what needed done.

More tanks and windmills were on my list. I was going after the horse stock I needed. Clarence had started on his plan to scatter the bulls. There were more of those situations that the cowboys had noticed, and I told Clarence to ask for them.

They'd all be improvements that would help. I wanted to build an impressive ranch. The job wouldn't be easy, but it could be great when I got through, and I aimed to do it.

Lex hitched to the wagon wheel, I rejoined Kate. Light was beginning to rise on the eastern horizon. The great disc would soon be up over east Texas.

"I'm getting closer." She smiled at me and picked up the coffee pot with a potholder and poured us some in tin cups.

I squatted on my boot heels. "No rush. We'll get there."

"Have you seen their horses?"

"One's out there with the team. The other two must be hid over east."

The coffee tasted good. She was making pancakes and about had a stack started. I sat down cross-legged on the ground and watched her work. There was nothing lethargic about her. I had thought she was slow. Maybe she was too bashful in my presence. But no one could have asked for a more organized woman at getting things done—on guard or being a cook—than she was. I damn sure never knew her plans for having me, anyway.

We ate in silence. I bragged on her food, and she shook her head. "I always please you."

"Hey, because no one ever bragged on you before, it ain going to keep me from thanking you."

"Good. I get embarrassed a little, I guess. I plan to do like said, always please you."

"Our life is going to be more of it, too." Saliva ran in my mouth as I chewed on the cakes. I was living high as usua eating with her, even on this battlefield that those outlaws ha made of our camp. But their efforts to ruin our honeymoo still made me seethe with anger.

Our meal over, she planned to wash the dishes, and I wer in the new light to find their horses. They were grazing togeth in a draw, and I brought them and our team back to camp. The

I went through the two dead men's pockets. They had less than forty dollars and a few letters I would read later. Nothing much else in their saddlebags. She came and helped me load the bodies over their saddles. We secured them with their lariats, harnessed ours, and I hitched them to the buckboard.

I learned the wounded one's name was Ethan Stone.

"I can make you one deal, Stone. You can ride on the back of the buckboard on a pallet. But one bad move, and you'll be riding belly down like those other two. What's your choice?"

"I'm dying."

"Make a choice. I ain't got all day."

"Buck. . . board."

I took two of their bedrolls and made him a pallet as she finished loading all her things. Then she took his feet, and I took his arms, and we hoisted him on the back. He did lots of moaning and pleading. We simply ignored him.

The team ready, she drove, and I rode Lex, leading their three horses. The temperature grew hotter as the day went on. After midday we reached a small town and reined up. When we stopped in front of the mercantile, a deputy must have saw the two bodies over their saddles and came on the run.

"What the hell is going on here?"

"These three and another man raided our camp last night. One got away."

"How bad off is he?" The young man gave a head toss toward Stone.

"Bad enough he needs a doctor." I helped Kate down. "My name is Gil Slatter. This is my wife, Kate. I'm foreman of the TXY Ranch in Evergreen County, Texas."

"Deputy Ira Newels, sir. I'll send a boy for the doc. These three look like tough characters. Who was the other one got away—do you know his name?"

"Ray Cline. You know him?"

"No, sir, but I'll look for him."

"I think he's their leader. They stopped by our camp about dark, and I talked to him then. Early thirties, light colored hair, wore an old hat had an eagle feather in it, but he wasn't a breed. Stone said he led them."

"We don't have much trouble up here. They stopped and talked to you?"

"Asked me about a ferry on the Red. I told them there used to be one. They rode on, but I told my wife they'd be back. We took shifts guarding our camp. They came back after midnight on foot, sneaking up on us."

"Gosh, sounds tough. Three men shot. There still is a ferry up there. Nigger Jim runs it. He don't have much traffic, anymore, but it feeds him."

"I have business to do at Fort Sill and a ranch to get back to and run. Let's get this over with."

"Oh, I'll get my boss." He hurried off.

I turned to our prisoner, who was moaning. "Where were you guys going?"

"He said. . . there was a payroll to steal. . . at the fort."

"And you all tried to steal a buckboard from a honeymooning couple?"

"He thought you were rich."

"Oh, very rich." I shook my head.

The sheriff was still buttoning his clothes as he came down the street in a stiff walk talking to his man.

"Hank tells me you're in a hurry. I'm Samuel Tyler. Hmm. Two dead men. Have they sent for Doc?"

"Yes, sir. He ain't made it yet. I'm on my honeymoon. I have business in Fort Sill. These outlaws tried to kill us. I can't stay here all day."

"Ma'am howdy. Sorry Mister...?"

"Gil Slatter."

"I need a secretary to take notes here. This is major crime for around here."

"Go get him. My wife and I plan to leave shortly. Is there a café here?"

"Three doors down. Miss Dooly can feed you."

"We'll go catch some lunch and then I want this business closed up. I have places to be. You have the criminals. Come on, Kate."

"He sure isn't much of a sheriff," Kate whispered as we headed for the café.

"This sure ain't much of a place, either. What was the name of it?"

"Clemency."

"That figures." I held the door open for her, and a bell rang overhead.

"Come in, come in. How are you folks today? Nice to have you two in town. Thinking of settling here, are you?"

"No, ma'am. We're on our honeymoon and headed for Fort Sill."

The short woman in her forties stopped and blinked at me. "You're on your honeymoon and going to Fort Sill? Why, most people run away from that place."

"I am buying some horses up there."

"Oh, they may have some of them. Sit right here. Lunch or breakfast?"

"Lunch," I said, and Kate nodded.

"Meatloaf, new potatoes, gravy, and green beans."

"Sounds fine. We both drink coffee—black."

"Coming up."

We left Clemency shortly after our two-bit lunches. Sheriff never asked if I found any money on them. I didn't need their sorry horses or saddles. I drove out with my horse hitched on the tailgate. They owed us that money for disturbing our honeymoon.

We crossed the ferry. The ancient black man reeled us across on his barge, and I paid him forty cents. He said my man, Ray Cline, swam the river. Too cheap to pay him twenty cents. I wished he'd drown doing that.

Two more days, and we were at Fort Sill. I spoke with the army man in charge of the desk and also spoke to the Indian agent's secretary. Both said I could trade with whoever I wanted, so I went to the trading post and spoke to the owner.

"Let me get this right," the whiskered man behind the counter said. "You want to buy two- to four-year-old geldings and hire some boys to take them back to Texas."

"That's my plan."

"I'll get the word out. I can rent you some corrals out back to hold them. Hay is ten bucks a ton."

"How much is the rent?"

"Thirty bucks."

"I'd pay twenty."

"You've got a deal."

So by nightfall, they were bringing in horses for me to look at. The first man brought three on light steel chains. Guess he ran out of rope. Wearing an unblocked hat with an eagle feather, he squatted by the corral while I checked them out.

The bay was too thin. The sorrel had a few scars, but none of them impeded his movement. He was near four. I figured he would be a tough one to break. His paint horse acted wall-eyed, but he was three. Cowboys hated paints, but this was a real horse. He'd do. They'd all like him after they rode him a day.

The man's name was Booth. Johnny Booth was what he called himself.

"How much for the red horse?"

"Twenty."

"Ten dollars for each. You keep the bay. He's too thin made."

"The bay is young."

"No, I need real horses."

He rose and held out his hand. "That bay is a good horse."

"I want the red and the paint. Twenty for both of them."

Booth shook his head. "You won't buy many horses here."

"That's all I can pay."

"I want my chains back."

"No problem. Let's put them in the corral." I settled with him, and he left still complaining I wouldn't buy many horses there.

When we woke up, I found he was way wrong. There must have been thirty people with horses already there to sell me stock when we got up in the predawn.

I told them I was there to buy horses— two to four years old and sound. No mares. I could see several had mares, and they left disappointed. I ate breakfast next. It would be a long day, and a cavalry sergeant came by to visit with me while I ate. His name was Nickolas Carwowskie. We had a nice talk about things.

By noon I had bought ten more, and the seller line grew longer. With pencil and paper, Kate kept an accurate track of my purchases.

I had put a fresh bought dun horse in the pen when three wild looking youths rode up and asked for work. They wore headbands with feathers in them

"You need herders?" the oldest one asked, reining his horse around to show me how broke he was.

"Tonight, I'll talk to you. We'll see who can ride these Co-manche ponies then."

They left with a war whoop. They might make good ones, but they'd have to have cowboy hats on to ride down through Texas. Texicans would not take to letting war-like Injuns ride that far down in their state even if they were working for me.

Horse trading continued, and I had thirty head of great cow pony prospects by sundown. The old man said for me to buy forty, and we could sell some to pay for the rest. Not a bad idea, either. It wasn't going to be long until I'd have them bought at that rate.

After supper, I had a dozen teenage boys sitting in a circle that were looking for work. Kate'd fed them her boiled frijoles and sweet cornbread, and I knew she was watching for the athletes in the outfit.

"My ranch is a two weeks' ride south of here," I said. "I want to get home with all my horses. You'll ride a different one each day. I'll feed you and pay you ten dollars in cash when we get there. Then you can ride home on your own horses."

Two of them got up, shook their heads. "That's not enough money."

"How much do you expect?" I asked.

"Thirty dollars."

I shook my head. "I'll pay fifteen dollars and food going down there."

They sat down. There was no other money-making deal fo them at the Fort.

"But you must wear cowboy hats, or I fear someone migh shoot you down there."

They laughed and agreed.

A dozen boys was too many, but not if they took the edge ol the broncs for my crew. In two weeks, those ponies would be rid den about every other day. I still had not spent too much mone So in the end I had fifteen riders and Little Joe, an orphan, t herd the forty loose horses.

In three days, they had all but the rowdy ones tamed a lot. used three of their horses to pack the grub we needed becaus Kate said we'd need more food for that hungry bunch before w got home. With packsaddles on three of them, Joe watched an made sure they came along with the loose ones. She drove th buckboard, and I rode Lex. We made good time. I quit in ear afternoon to water and graze them each day. The boys helpe her get meals ready, and found wood for her to cook with.

The sheriff at Clemency said he'd not seen the fourth ma

when we passed through there. The third outlaw had died so there would be no trial. The lawman could not believe the quality of the horses I'd bought from the Comanche. And how I had them damn near broke going home by my men riding them.

It rained that evening, and everyone stayed on a deserted place in an old barn that shed water. We had enough raincoats for the nighthawks. Kate and I were in the sidewall tent on cots up off the wet ground. We only used one bed and laughed about bringing two. Those crazy boys had her laughing about something all day long.

"Neatest honeymoon a girl could ask for. My sides hurt from laughing so much. I never knew Indians could be that much fun."

"And even that ornery sorrel horse is damn near broke to ride."

We finally went off to sleep. Still was some thunder in the night, but nothing wild. Next morning, those boys had her fire going, and everyone was hustling around to get the packhorses loaded. Mounts were saddled, and with her cooking going on, the boys took down the tent and cots to load. Her team was hitched. I was damn sure they were the best hustlers I'd ever seen in a stock driving outfit.

CHAPTER 4

I decided we'd drive the horses right through the two blocks of businesses downtown in Dog Springs. Be good to advertise my horse sale coming up. The word was out where I'd went, and I was sure it was getting spread all over. I told those boys to do some fancy riding going through town. Besides, Eagle Hand jumping clear over Claude Knowles's buckboard on the big paint, and the others riding off on the side of their mounts like they were attacking Indians, they got the herd through town with a free wild west show. Kate sure laughed about it, driving her buckboard through behind them.

We reached the ranch about sundown. Clarence came to greet me and nodded his approval at the horses. "Which one's ours?"

"They're riding a part of them."

Clarence shook his head in disbelief, realizing I'd got them broncs green-broke coming down.

The cook said he could feed us, so we corralled them all and went to have supper. Norman flirted with Kate, and made a big fuss over her eating with him.

I heard her say, "As long as I don't have to fix it, it will be fine with me."

For privacy, the boys set up our tent for the two of us to sleep in that night. I gave them the word that I'd pay them after breakfast and they could go home. After the morning meal the next day, I counted out eighteen dollars for each, saying the three was a bonus. They grinned in line and nodded their approval. In an hour my young riders were gone north for home with some food in tow sacks to eat on the way.

Clarence and I went over the horses in the pens. Five of them still needed some hard riding, but they were amazingly tame. Then I went to the big house and reported to the boss.

"Got forty horses. Cost under twenty bucks apiece," I told the old man, handing him a copy of the figures.

"How many?"

"Forty."

"They as good as they looked from up here?"

"They're better than that."

"I understand you broke them coming down."

"Those boys rode all of them."

He shook his head in dismay. "What do you want for the spare ones?"

"Eighty dollars apiece."

"Ten at that price will pay for them. You're high priced."

"I don't need to sell them. But if anyone wants a real horse, they're cheap."

"I heard you put on a real show coming through Dog Springs yesterday."

"One of those boys jumped that paint over a man's buckboard."

The old man shook his head amused. "Nice job. Those three

bulls are split up, and they brought in and shod that Hereford bull you talked about. Clarence thinks he'll recover."

"My men don't need me standing over them. Clarence has close to fifty barren cows marked with paint, but there's more, so we can cut them out when we find a market for them."

He nodded. "You've got an eye for the job. What about Kate? She looks fired up."

"She's tough as any man. We had some folks tried to rob and kill us up there on the road. She put one of them down with my .45."

He nodded. "She was raised tough. Like a boy, but I can see the gleam in her eye around here with you. Good luck to you two. How many good cows we got today?"

"I've looked in his books. I need to start over on them. I bet we have over two hundred barren cows eating our grass."

"That many?"

"Maybe more than that. He hasn't culled any in years. They get old, no teeth, and die in the winter."

"We'll bridge it. I trust you. I want to see you sell ten of those Comanche broncs for eighty bucks apiece. I'll laugh all night."

"Hell, you like to make money."

"I make money, you will, too. You and Kate go home and take a few days off. You've pulled a good deal here."

"I'll see. I want those hands to ride those horses a lot. I want them real broke in the next month."

The old man sent me on and congratulated me in a damn good humor about my job when I left him. That was a change.

Before I left, me and Clarence hunkered down by the corral. My plan was for each man to take two of the horses and ride them each two days out of a week. They'd soon find the sour and unbroken ones. Plus ride the good ones into town on Saturday night and show them off on the hitch rack. I wanted to sell ten of them to make his plan work.

I took Kate home that evening in the buckboard. She was snuggled against me in a good mood.

"We're going to the dance Saturday night. You want to make a dress?" I said.

"Of course. And you are going to get stepped on."

"I don't mind. I think you'll catch on fast."

"I'm scared."

"Aw, hell, dancing ain't bear hunting. It's having fun."

She shook her head with a face of dread. "I'd rather bear hunt. I can shoot better than step around."

"Who's got a guitar up here?"

"Henny plays one."

"Get him to bring it over, and we can practice before we go."

"That's not a bad idea."

The next morning, my first appraisal of her gardening operation was she needed a windmill.

We were both using hoes to catch the new weeds in her near-perfect garden. "How much water is in that well?"

"It never has gone dry. Why?"

"You need a windmill to irrigate it."

She kinda squinted at me like I was tetched in the head. "They cost lots of money."

"Oh, I bet we can find one used."

"How much will it cost?"

I leaned on my hoe to catch my breath. "Oh, a hundred or hundred and fifty. Plus with a mill, you wouldn't have to hand pump that shower barrel full."

"I'd like that. Who has the money?"

"I have the money."

"Oh, I hate—"

"No, what I have, you have. We'll hook up the buckboard tomorrow and go find one."

She mopped the sweat from her face with a flour sack,

then did my wet face the same. "There. We can quit at the end of this row of corn."

"Thanks."

"I try to do this early every day."

"Good. It's been getting hotter and hotter every day. Summer's coming fast."

When we reached the end, I took the hoe from her to put up. "There's a nice spring hole up at Fisher's Springs. No one lives up there anymore. We can go soak up there and be cool. Do you want to ride up there and cool off?"

"Sure. I'll fix us something to eat, and we can stay past dark."

"Great idea. I'll saddle some horses."

"I never thought being married to you would be so much fun."

She had a shift she wore to swim in. And she could swim too. When her dress was wet, you could see her through it, but I knew she felt more secure with something on in case someone rode up. We ate her tortilla-bean roll-ups for supper, and didn't leave the hole till the moon came up.

Riding home beside me, she threw her head back and whistled loud. "Funnest day of my life, Gil Slatter. I never took a day off in my entire life. Just to swim and play. You're really spoiling me."

"I never had anyone to take a half-day off and picnic with me."

"What's tomorrow?"

"Find a windmill day."

"Oh, yes. Wind power."

Me and Kate rode most of the day from here to there looking for one for sale. Late afternoon, we found a man who had two used ones. His name was Ed Carney. They were lying on their sides at his place and looked workable. After two hours dickering, he agreed to sell me one and set it up. He also had two iron tanks that he'd set up and would also pipe the shower tank so Kate didn't have to fill it by buckets. Total cost—a hundred-twenty bucks. Him and two men would deliver it the next evening. They'd stay overnight and install it the next day. Tank setups might take a few days longer, since they needed to be on wooden stands.

The stars filled the sky as me and Kate rode home that evening.

"Let me see—I will have water at the shower and at my back door. Then a setup to irrigate my garden when the tanks are full. Oh my, Mr. Slatter, I'm going to be spoiled, that's for sure. Why, in hot summers, I watered that garden with a bucket that I pumped full each time." She leaned way back in her saddle and rode her horse in circles around mine. "I don't know how to take it."

I laughed at her antics. "Somehow you'll figure it out." I never knew if it was those days with the Comanche boys that did that to her or me, but she was getting a wild sense of humor the farther we went down the road. No, for once in her life she was free to be Kate—no holds barred. Riding home that night to the crickets' symphony and the coyotes howling, I was smugly happy. A feeling that I'd never had since I was that boy growing up in Texas. I could please her and I'd learned I could even please the old man. Not bad.

The windmill setup had a loud clack when it spun, even though it was well greased. But it could sure pump water on the wind that came out of Mexico about fifty miles south of us. My lands, her garden flourished, too. That season we bought a big lot of the Mason jars to can for harder times. I had to shore up the shelves in her cellar so they didn't collapse under the weight of them.

We damn sure wouldn't starve as things really came on in the garden with the water. I told her that joke about water and the Arizona Territory, how the guy told some folks all he needed was water. And the guy said, "Yeah, they said the same damn thing about Hell."

My plans for the big ranch were developing. Clarence and I had done some well drilling up in the foothills with a rig I bought cheap from a man quitting the business. Clarence made some repairs to it, and in two days' drilling we hit our first artesian well. I took three cowboys, draft horses, and some slips up there to catch it in a tank we hastily hollowed out to hold it.

The next week I took the old man up there in his buckboard. He couldn't believe what we'd done.

"That water is simply coming out of the ground." He looked amazed at the level already in the new tank.

"I heard there was artesian water available at the base of some of these ranges. We may not find another, but this one will supply an area where we only had stock water when it rained up here."

"Why, that ain't even legal." The old man laughed so hard he went to coughing.

"I want to start a drilling gang to make more wells. And the men can cap it so we can shut it down after we get enough water in the tank."

"Four men?"

"Maybe five, counting a boy to help them."

"I can't argue with that."

"Good. I have them drilling up the way already. They had some traces yesterday, and may hit it today."

The old man shook his head. "How long you been figuring on all this?"

"Since you made me the foreman."

The old man shook his head in disbelief. "Bullshit, you've been looking at these things ever since you came here."

"You know what I think? Jeff Horne is coming next week to buy those ten horses."

"By God, I believe you. Gil, you're special."

That trip out to the well about wore him out, but it also made him sit up next time when I came by the house to see him.

"Did you sell the horses?" Kate asked me when I arrived over there for my weekend with her.

I hugged and kissed her and bobbed my head. "Yes, he took ten of them, and said he wanted more when I went back."

"You going back?"

"I may have to."

"Can I go?"

"Hell, yes."

"Whoopee. I've got that new dress made for Saturday night."

"Hell, we can run up there and swim in that water hole tonight."

She was hugging and kissing me like a wild woman. "Never a dull time with you, big guy."

I couldn't have bought her anything that made her happier than my offer to go swim.

We took some jerky to chew on and some fresh tomatoes from her garden to eat while we rode up there. The spring water fed into the pool. She brought a thick blanket for us to sit on the bank when we came out. Bathing and swimming in the hole was relaxing, and we kissed a lot until she whispered, "We need to use the blanket."

I looked around as the sun set—no one to be seen. Pleased with her suggestion, I hugged her tight. "You're the light of my life."

"Or maybe your shady lady, huh?"

"Everything a man could ask for." I nuzzled on her neck. "You can't believe how much I miss you over there."

"Oh, we can always catch up on that." She snuggled against me in her thin wet gown.

On the bank, she shed her garment and joined me. Side by side we kissed until she told me to get up, and she slipped over to take me in her arms on top of her. When I moved, I realized there was lots less of her than my initial visit. How had I not noticed that about her before then?

My discovery made me smile. How would I tell her I was proud of her efforts and not say it wrong? No time to think about it—I had lots of pleasure at hand. I kissed her and enjoyed the building excitement—damn, how lucky could a man get? My life was so full of great things like having sex with a woman who adored me. I enjoyed every minute of our engagement with each other. My mind swirled as our pace increased, and I grew wilder and hotter until the climax came from the depth of my manhood, where exploded and sent me out of the world I lived in. We both about fainted.

"Can I ask you something?" she whispered.

"Sure darling."

"I'm learning lots about being married. I thought people only did this like animals to make babies. But there is much more to it than that, isn't there?"

"You're right, darling. I can't get over the excitement we have doing it and then how it leaves me so relaxed I'm limp." I kissed her.

"Well not too limp." She laughed.

I lifted myself onto my knees. "Thanks for the rug. It was a neat part. Let's go swim some more and then go home. I like the bed even better."

She did not put her garment back on when she went in the water. Good, she was relaxing more about things around us. Hell, besides two coyotes and a dozen range cows and calves waiting for a drink, there was no one to see her naked, anyway.

Out of the water, we dried and dressed.

"I never checked—is your windmill working good?"

She paused to kiss me. We did that a lot.

"It's doing wonderful," she sighed. "I'm so spoiled I don't know how things could be any better. We have plenty of food in the cellar, and lots more to put up."

"Baby, I never dreamed I needed a wife so bad. You're perfect for me."

"I told you I dreamed about. . . well, having you for a mate, but I never dreamed I'd. . . well, be swept off my feet. This has been a crazy dust devil for me to ride inside of."

"I need to go to Fort Worth and find a cattle buyer pretty soon. It isn't a great place, but I want you along to see it."

"I don't need to go along."

"Stop being the invisible one with that little girl voice. You're my wife, and I want you to see what I see and the rest. Besides that, I am damn proud you're my wife."

She tackled me. Tears ran down her face. I hugged her, then went to put the horses up. After that, we went off to bed. Not for sleep, but to bed.

CHAPTER 5

he potluck and dance was at the Whittaker schoolhouse, a few hours' drive over east. We took the buckboard. Kate fixed up dinner and dessert. I had the tent, two cots, and some cooking gear for breakfast, plus groceries and Arbuckle coffee. The drive was through lots of open range cedar and live oak country and over some small hills. There were plenty of rigs already there when I pulled up and spoke to a man chewing on a straw and wearing overalls

"Is there a special place to park?"

He looked around from under his straw hat. "No, I don't reckon there is. Make yourself at home. My name's Pete Crawford."

"This my wife, Kate. I'm Gil Slatter."

"I heard of you."

"I'm the new foreman for the old man on the TXY."

"You got any more of them good horses for sale?"

"What would you give for one?"

"Hundred and a half for a damn good one."

"What color?"

"Blood bay. Black hooves."

I thought for a minute. "I have one, but he's worth two hundred."

Not too bad shaken by my price, the old man chewed on his straw. "Broke?"

I knew he was going to bite. "Broke good enough to ride."

"Bring him next week. I have the money."

"Be glad to, Mr. Crawford. Drive them over there, Kate," I directed, trying not to bust I was so damn excited about my sale.

She was suppressing a big smile. I waved to the man and hurried after her. She had climbed off the seat in her new blue dress, and I took off the tugs. I leaned over and whispered. "Wait till I tell the old man."

"I know. You're a tough guy to deal with in a trade, and I love you."

She straightened up and made sure my buyer was gone.

"That will be the highest priced horse ever sold around here."

"Yes. We may have to go back to Fort Sill. I wanted to wait till fall when it was cooler. Those Indians still have lots of good horses."

"What the damn army didn't kill."

"Yes, they killed lots of them. I heard about that. Some say thousands. Soldiers got so damn tired killing them they cried."

"But it makes them scarce."

I got our horses unharnessed and hitched, then set up the tent. By then, some curious kids arrived. Kate enlisted some of the youths to help her carry her food inside the schoolhouse to the long table. A few drove tent stakes for me, and in no time it was up and the cots set inside.

"You're the man with the high priced horses?" a blond-headed boy asked.

"Yes. You need one?"

The boy blushed and turned up his hands. "I don't have no money, mister."

"What is your name?"

"Cord Bentson."

"Mine's Gil."

"I knowed, yeah."

"Good, where do you live?"

"I don't got no place."

"Where are your parents?"

"Dead."

"Where do you live then?"

"Oh, anywhere that folks will let me stay." The boy shrugged.

"You don't go to school?"

"Naw, I kin read and count."

"You need a job?"

He blinked his eyes at me. "You have a job?"

"I have a place over west. Needs a lot of work. I'd pay ten dollars a month and board."

"What do I got to do if I get that job?"

"Cut and split wood. Plow a garden. Dig up stumps."

"I can do that."

"Be here in the morning. We'll have breakfast, and you can go home with us."

"I'll be here."

"Good."

I watched the boy saunter off. Had I done it right? I'd know in no time at all.

Inside, I joined Kate on the bench along the wall.

"You find a pretty girl to flirt with?"

"No." I about laughed. "I hired a boy to help you."

She frowned and looked at me.

"Cord Bentson came by. He's in his teens. He's an orphan."

"Where is he?"

"I told him to be ready to go in the morning."

She looked hard at me. "He has no one?"

"That's what he said."

She straightened up and glanced down at her hands. "I hope he isn't a murderer."

"He just looks like a boy that needs some assistance."

"We will see, won't we?"

The crowd was growing inside. I had been there before as a single guy and danced with some ladies, but that had been over a year ago. When the music started, we rose and started dancing. Kate was a little stiff, but she soon loosened up, and I had her going around the floor.

"See what I told you?" I said.

She looked up and smiled at me as we all shuffled around. "Now I can do more than shoot outlaws with my husband."

"Kate, that doesn't sound good at all." I hardly could keep down my amusement. We retired to the bench.

"I'm sorry. I was learning how to dance, and I thought that was something better." She had to laugh. "You're way too serious tonight."

"I'll watch that closer."

"Oh, I never had anyone to tease in my life." She leaned on me with two hands clasped on my shoulder.

"Hey, I think they're going to let us eat."

"Good. Maybe I will be excused."

"Excused?"

"Never mind." She produced two tin plates and silverware wrapped in a towel.

Someone said grace. Everyone was standing and said amen. We met more people in the line. They remarked about our marriage and wished us well. One man asked about my horse sales.

"Yes, sir, I will have some more in the fall."

"I heard you sold one tonight?"

"I did. You need a horse?"

"Will he be like those ten you sold a week or so ago?"

"One of that lot. They are three to four years old. What color?"

"A sorrel?"

"I can bring him next Friday night. He don't suit you, I'll take him home."

"What will I owe you?"

"Two hundred dollars."

The man whistled. He was on opposite side of the table behind his wife filling his plate.

I looked over at him for an answer.

"Bring him." At his words his wife twisted around and gave him a cutting look.

I was almost afraid my wife would mock him, but she didn't. But I had gone past the dessert by mistake. Guess selling two horses that high priced had me shook. We were back by ourselves on the wall bench, each tasting ten different dishes we'd piled on our plates.

"That old man needs to start paying you to come to these events."

"Yeah, and he may have a coughing fit when I tell him what I've done."

"Oh, yes, you said it was serious. You didn't get any of the white cake, did you?" She raised a little to look over there. "I bet it's all gone. I saw someone brought a bowl of stewed prunes. You may still get some of that—" She went to laughing.

I did too. "I never knew you could laugh like that."

"No? Well, now I'm crying." She buried her face in my shoulder.

"You ain't the only one. Prunes, bah."

That made another round of laughing. I gave her my handkerchief to wipe her face, and we had to settle down to eat more.

Clarence showed up by himself. Since the bench was full, he squatted down and started eating off his full plate. "I want to know what was so damn funny and how I missed it."

"Oh, he sold another horse to a man in line, and was so dang shook and busy he missed getting any dessert. So I told him there might be some stewed prunes left over there when he goes back."

Clarence went to laughing and had to hold himself up with his free hand to keep from sprawling out on the floor. Kate and me were back to cackling.

She straightened up and turned to him. "I never really thanked you, but I do love your grandma's ring."

"Hell, you kissed his face off for it," I said.

That brought more laughter, and she shook her head but couldn't get out of laughing herself.

"Damn, Gil I see why you married her. Why, she'd tickle the ribs off an old sourpuss, wouldn't she?"

"Poor me." I said. "The things I must put up with."

Clarence's eyes were still wet. "What I came to tell you was the guys caught that last big longhorn bull that hung around up there on the Burro Flats and he's a steer today."

"Why, we've chased him for years. He broke more riatas than any of them. How did they do that?"

"Using one of them good stout horses you brung down from Fort Sill. They got him lined out, and Perkins came in, roped him, then rode right past him—can you imagine— then threw that rope over his butt and turned hard left. It was some crash, and in no time they had him tied up, worked, and branded. We never before had a ranch horse that could run past him to put the rope over his butt."

"No. That big devil always busted the rope or drug down some horses."

An old fellow came over to us. "You TXY boys are having too much fun down here. Howdy ma'am." He tipped his hat to Kate and showed off his gray head of hair.

"Kate, meet Elmer George. He ramrods the Five Star Ranch."

"I've met Kate before. But she wasn't wearing your brand back then. Sorry I was out of pocket when your father died, ma'am."

"That was fine," she said.

"Best of luck to both of you. I never got an invite in the mail."

"We didn't have a big wedding," I said to him.

"You have any of those high-priced horses left?"

"I can get some," I said. "Twenty, thirty head?"

"No. I know where they came from."

"You better be careful going up there after them," she said. "We got raided on by four white outlaws. We killed three of them."

He tipped his hat to her. "Have fun. I better go see a man."

"That's one guy I hate. He knows it, too," she said with a frown.

"I guess so. You had your teeth clenched talking to him."

"I'll tell you later." She shook her head ruefully.

"Fine. Clarence, he always wants to run over somebody, doesn't he?"

"Hell, you scooped him on selling them horses. He don't like to be beat at nothing."

She moved to the edge of the bench. "If you ain't going for them prunes, give me your plates and silverware. I'll go wash both of your services and be back."

I stood up for her, and so did Clarence. She took them and went to a tub of hot soapy water with another tub next to it to rinse.

Clarence waited till she was beyond hearing. "That wife of yours ain't got any use for old George for some reason."

"I read the same damn thing you did. I'll find out later."

"Hey, bring my tin plate to work Monday. I know an old boy keeps some hooch outside, and I need a little to get up my nerve to ask some gal to dance."

"Thanks. She really did appreciate that ring. Me, too."

"I'm damn glad she's wearing it. I won't ever need it. Have fun."

"Monday morning. Oh, I did sell a bay and a sorrel here tonight for two hundred apiece."

Clarence frowned in disbelief. "Hell, we won't have any good horses left at that rate."

"There are still more."

"Wonder what the old man will say?"

"She said he'd have a coughing fit."

"Yeah, that, too. See you. Thanks, Kate," he said as he passed her going to the door.

We danced some more and finally turned in. There was lots going on outside around the two big bonfires. Most of that involved drinking. In the flickering light, Clarence had his arm around some brassy looking woman.

Once we got to the tent, Kate closed the front opening and tied it. Getting up from her task, she smiled in the light coming through canvas from the big fires.

"I did have a good time tonight dancing with you. I never thought I would, but I was amazed at how sweet it is to be in your arms anyway."

She sat down on the edge of the couch and unhooked her shoes.

"I'm proud of you, Kate. You're a doer and try hard. Tell me about George. Somewhere he stepped on your tail. Even Clarence saw that."

"You know I lived alone. Many times dad never even came home on the weekends. George showed up one time, and I knew he wasn't there to see dad—it was mid-week. He told me how much he loved me and we should get together. I asked him about his wife. He dismissed that—he wanted me."

In her silence, I waited.

"Then he got pushy, and I tried to avoid him. He pushed me on the bed and began kissing me like I'd swoon or something. Somehow I got his gun out of his holster and cocked it. He backed up, begging me not to shoot him. I told him never to come back, or I'd meet him at the door and shoot him with my shotgun."

"He left?"

"He left after that. I'll show you his gun when we get home. I still have it, and he knows I do."

"Hell, Kate, I don't doubt you one minute. A wonder you didn't shoot me."

In the dim light, she pursed her lips and shook her head. "I wanted you."

We both laughed.

"I'm sorry if I offended you earlier. But it was off the top of my brain when I asked were you flirting outside."

"Last thing on my mind, that's for sure." I barely recalled what she'd said.

"Oh, Gil, I am so happy. I've been a stay-at-home all my life. You've not only taken me down another path, but I really appreciate you all the time."

"Let's get undressed."

"I'm ready. You don't need to defend my honor over George. He never got anything but a smothered kiss and squeezed my breast. That's been maybe two years ago. He's never been back, but acts so gawdamn superior I can't stand him."

"He is a little above the rest, and me selling those high priced horses has him pissed off, too. He thinks he knows it all."

"But he don't." She stood up and shed her dress, laughing all the time.

She put on a sleeping gown, and we were soon on the cot facing each other. She swept her hair back. "I don't know why I put this gown on. But you're handy enough you can work around it and still find me."

I laughed and snuggled closer.

If I'd ever found a great woman, she was there with me in bed. Thank God, it sure beat anything I ever imagined. I'd even the score with George, too, for what he did to her.

CHAPTER 6

Sunday morning, Cord was sitting on the ground when I came out of the tent to empty my bladder. I nodded and said back to Kate, "Our company is here."

"Fine."

"Rest easy," I said to him. "We're getting it together."

"Thanks."

When I came back, he had a small fire setup in a ring. "I need a match."

I found one and handed it to him. The cedar shavings began to blaze after he torched it. When I turned, she came outside and nodded her approval at his work.

"Cord, that's my wife, Kate."

He jumped up and took off his hat. "Yes, ma'am, I am sure glad to meet you."

She glanced at the rolled up blanket and small sack. "That all you have with you to move?"

"I told Mr. Slatter that I had nothing or no one."

She nodded, and handed him the grill to go over the fire. "I can handle it now."

"Yes, ma'am. You need more wood. I can get it."

"Looks like there's enough here. Thanks."

"Good. I'm looking forward to working for both of you."

"We are, too." She put the coffee pot on to boil, then had him fill the pot with water from the pump for her to make oatmeal with. I finished dressing and joined her.

"He's awful thin, isn't he?" she said, a concerned look in her eyes.

"You can fatten him up."

"I can try. You know where he's lived?"

I squatted down on my boot heels to feel some of the heat from the fire in the dawn coolness. "No, he'll have to tell us."

"I guess we will have to learn over time."

I agreed.

She had lots of brown sugar and raisins for the oatmeal to stir in when the water and oats had boiled. On her feet, she poured us coffee. Cord didn't need either sugar or evaporated milk in his. I felt that was a sign he'd been in a place where he was lucky to even get coffee, period.

He and I took down the tent and cots. Two more men stopped by and asked when I'd get some more horses. I said we planned to go back in the fall and would advertise when they were available. They thanked me. I let Cord harness the team. He did a good job.

After a hearty breakfast and coffee, we loaded the rest. He rode home with us in the back of the buckboard.

At the ranch, he acted impressed while he helped me put things up. Then he unharnessed the team. We spent the rest of the day cleaning out a shed for him sleep in. We found him an iron cot and a mattress, plus three quilts. It was a fair place to bunk in, and Cord acted pleased.

Kate showed him the woodpile she had hired cut and had delivered there. She told him to split it. She also had some lot fences needing repaired.

"I can handle it, Mrs. Slatter."

"I am Kate. I will have breakfast each morning, lunch at noon. Supper is late evening. Knock before you come in my house."

"Yes, ma'am."

"I have some magazines if you can read. It being Sunday, you don't need to work."

"I can read. Thanks."

We had lunch at noontime, and he came to the house. After that he thanked her and went back to read.

When he was gone, she frowned, "You know I am used to being here alone."

"You just will have to dress. No more naked hoeing the corn."

She shook her head. "I never do that, but I do need to be more aware."

"I think we can help him."

"I'm surprised you didn't bring me a floppy-eared pup."

"He's close to that."

We both laughed.

Early Monday morning, I took Clarence's tin plate and eating utensils back with me to the ranch. I left Cord splitting wood and my wife looking sad I was leaving her. I hoped the two reached an accord.

I met the crew and told them I sold a bay horse and sorrel for a large price. I needed the men to ride them hard that week. Two cowboys showed disappointed faces.

"Hey, our jobs count on this ranch making money. If I can sell ranch horses for two hundred dollars apiece, I have to sell them and go get some more."

The men nodded.

"I understand we finally got that old bull we have all chased for a long time. That's good work and proves my point, put good men on good horses, and you get results. Let's start easing those barren cows that we marked with paint in here. I have to find a market for them, but we need to assemble them. Now you all have things to check on. Let's get it done."

I waited till they was gone, then asked Clarence, "How's the drilling crew getting along?"

"They're pounding rock up north. That country around the base of the big bluff needs more stock water."

"Good place to drill."

"Anything else?"

I shook my head. "The bull situation getting better?"

"Yes, I saw that shod bull breed a cow last week. I never thought that would ever work. You learn new tricks, don't you?"

I agreed with a nod. My man was learning. I liked that. "I better go see if the old man's up."

"Later."

Up at the house, I found Grimes and Mandy in the kitchen.

"Pour him some coffee. What's happened?" The old man slurped his milky oatmeal off a spoon.

"Those boys roped that big tough longhorn bull last Friday and cut him."

"Boy, we should have had a bull ball." He chuckled.

I was amused. His cook frowned at the notion of his intention.

"I also sold two more horses over the weekend."

"Oh?"

"I figured at two hundred a head, they needed them more than we did."

"Wa-hoo!"

"I had some more ask about them, but I think it was too high for them."

He pounded the table with his small fist. "Now that's wheeling and dealing."

Mandy had to settle his coffee cup down. "Land's sake, you're going to make a mess."

"We sold twelve hundred dollars' worth of horses. Didn't you hear Slatter?"

She shook her head. "It sure ain't worth cleaning up a mess over."

I stepped in. "I plan to go back in the fall for more."

"Good. You're doing good. Kate all right?"

"Doing fine. She has a windmill to help her."

He frowned like I'd farted in the kitchen, giving her that for a wedding present. "A helluva gift for a woman. Tell her I said hi."

"I will, sir. I have some things to check on. I may wire some buyers in Fort Worth about these barren cows. We need them off our ranges."

"Good. You put paint on them?"

"Yes. I wanted them marked so we can start driving them in here."

"You think of lots of things. Good. You handle it."

To send a telegram, I had to ride into Dog Springs. That would eat up some time. But I had a list of buyers in Grimes's old office. I'd grab them and go on in to the telegraph office down there. I put the addresses in my saddlebags, told Norman, the cook, where I was going and said Clarence was in charge. For a mount, I picked that big paint horse out of the Comanche string and switched my saddle to him. To keep him from bucking me off before I had a seat, I held the bridle cheek strap on the left side pulled tight against my leg until my boots and spurs were settled in the stirrups. That made the paint circle around, and I realized with all the heads popping up around the ranch stead to see me do it this must be the tough one in the string.

I set him out, using the side of my spurs to nudge him on. He half-stepped, undecided. I had to shock him out of his tracks, so

I put the rowels to him and cross-whipped him with the leather reins and shouted, "Hee-yah."

Comanche went in the air like his legs were coil springs. But I had both hands on the reins, and he couldn't get his head low enough to really buck. That's when he headed for the crossbar over the gate.

Man, he was powerful, and this wasn't his first fling at trying to buck. He must have pitched several riders off in the past. But on the road I had his head up, and he walked on eggs.

I had won the first battle.

Then he wanted escape, and that meant run. So I sent him off, and if he thought he was going to outrun me, he should have thought again. But he could damn sure run. When he began to drop back on his speed, I spurred him and used the reins on him. We went by several folks in rigs who only saw our dust.

By the time I was halfway to town, I cut him down to a trot. His shoulders were covered in foamy sweat, and his breath raged in and out his throat. Bobbing his head up and down with his pace, he blew his nose clear several times.

What a magnificent horse, despite his damn bright colors. In my life I'd ridden some real broncs, but this big devil was the kind of horse you needed to rope the big cattle off of and tie on to a lead rope of a pony that won't lead. With a lariat rope tied to a chuck wagon tongue, he could drag a weak team and the wagon through a mud bath.

I was impressed when I dismounted at the telegraph office. But in case he might have a head tossing fit, I used a lariat to tie him to the hitch rail. With my papers, I went inside and composed my letter on their yellow sheet.

Dear Sir,
My name is Gil Slatter and I am the new ranch foreman for the TXY

Ranch. I have approximately two hundred sound older cows in good flesh I would like to move to market in the next sixty days. I can be contacted at Gil Slatter, Dog Springs, Texas.

I showed the telegrapher the list of names and addresses I wanted them sent to. He copied them down. When he finished, he calculated the bill as three dollars, fifty cents.

"I will pay a half dollar for any telegram delivered to me at the ranch headquarters."

"Why, I can get plenty of messengers for that."

"Good. Thanks."

Outside in the sun's heat, I decided to ride right back to the ranch and skip any food or beer in town. My ranch cook, Norman, would find me something to eat when I returned, since I stayed at the ranch all week and could only wonder how my wife and that boy were getting on. Kate could handle it. I'd learn everything Friday when I took the horses with me to deliver them.

One day down and four more to go. The big horse shortloped most of the way home, and the sun was set long before I got back to walking him the last mile to cool him out.

Clarence came up to take the reins. "Norman said you'd come back tonight. He's got food up there for you." Then he chuckled. "You cost some of our bunch some money today. They bet you couldn't ride this big paint devil under the crossbar."

"I bet they did. He's one helluva horse, but if I needed one—a tough one—he'd be the one I'd want."

Clarence laughed. "I didn't bet, but you made a helluva ride. What do you call him?"

"Comanche."

"That will do. I bet you wished you had a big can of paint for that horse."

"My thoughts exactly. I better get up there, or Norman will throw my supper out. Thanks for putting him up."

The older man that handled the chuck part was smoking his cob pipe in a captain's chair. He had a lamp on the end of one of the long tables where the crew ate. My food was there.

"Thanks." I shed my spurs before I got on the long bench. "I knew you'd take care of me."

"You're the boss. Even if you have a wife now, it's my job to feed you the rest of the time. I believe you're a fair man, and we needed you. This is a hell of a ranch, and I can already see you making it lots better."

"Speaking of better, I may drive a couple hundred cull cows up to the loading pens on the Fort Worth Denver Railroad at the Sparkle Switch. Have you got a man to handle the chuck wagon?"

"Ten days going, five coming back?"

"Yeah, I guess."

"It will take that. I can get that set up. Do you have a man that can cook for your crew?"

"I can find a good one." I was busy eating his beef and beans and nodding. "You're worth every penny he pays you. This food is good as usual. I'll keep you informed when I need to move."

He took out his pipe and yawned. "Turn out the light. I'll wash your dishes in the morning. Put them in the big bucket. I'm going to sleep."

"Do that. You have an early call. Thanks, too."

I finished the supper and the peach cobbler, then put the dishes up and blew out the light. My room was in the end of the bunkhouse with a private entry. It had its own stove for heat in winter and a desk still cluttered with Thorpe's things. I needed Kate to come over and see what she wanted to save. I had changed sheets and got new blankets when I moved in to sleep there.

There was enough starlight coming in the three windows to undress in the dark, and I was soon was in bed and ready to sleep. Been nice to have had her there to hug—hell. I just needed to get some sleep.

Next morning, I was up, dressed, and down in the dining room under the lights to eat with my crew. I filled my plate with eggs, side meat, biscuits, and flour gravy. That and good coffee would fix a cowhand up to make it through the day if he couldn't get back at noon. Those who wouldn't get back had some fried apple raisin pies to take along. Norman was a damn good ranch cook and the fussiest man about being clean.

Clarence and I rode out together for the drillers' location after he assigned the men to their tasks for the day.

"How are things going?"

"It's different. I tell a man I want something done, I guess I get a little short sometimes. I don't ask them to do anything I have not done myself. 'Get off your damn horse and straighten out the barbwire mess where some wild critter busted through it. We have those fences so you don't have to ride your ass off. They detour our stock from going west to hell knows where.' But I get some words back on how he'd hired on a cowboy, not a damn fence hand."

"I guess you got that clear to him."

"Damn right. We're doing what you asked me to do, cut out hiring folks to do small things we can do ourselves."

"My dad said folks will bitch about the damnedest things. I come to understand that when I had your job. They don't mean anything mad or bad. They just think they are being degraded."

"I'll remember that. Can I ask, are you happy as you first were with Kate?"

"More so by the day. She and I fit together doing things, and we are having lots of fun. Hell, I'd forgot how to laugh."

"Prunes and all?"

"Yeah. She finds those little things, and they're funny. Poor girl never was hugged or kissed in her life, and she's making up for it with me."

"You ever think about having your own ranch some day?"

"Clarence, it would be tough to get it all together. To buy a place, get the horses and cattle, bulls, and the money to meet expenses. I've thought about it, and it worries me, things like drought, bad cattle prices, even disease all make me think I'll just get my small place fixed up to care for us if anything happens and try to work till I have to retire."

"That's a long ways down the road."

"Some days it isn't as far as you think."

Clarence agreed.

The drillers were pounding away. So far not any moisture, but the headman Tye said, "That don't mean anything. You can break through some rock formation and have it filled in no time."

Tye told his helper, Mike, to hold on to the cable. It was a driller's job to stop the pounding if the bit got wedged down in the well. Caught down there, it could break the cable if it was wedged too solid when the unit pulled it up to drop again. If the bit was caught they had to release it instantly.

Tye took us over to where he had samples of the material they were currently drilling in. "See this blue clay?"

Both Clarence and I agreed we could see it.

Tye grinned. "That first artesian well showed this material before we opened it up."

"Man, that would be something to have two of those wells," I said, impressed with his method of keeping track of the material he drilled in.

"You know those layers under the earth are not on smooth planes down there. The earth has shifted and piled some on top of other layers, so we may not have anything, but I feel we're close."

"You need anything up here?" I asked.

"No, we get our food on Monday, and we get enough. Your man is very helpful to us, too. Our equipment that Clarence overhauled and fixed is running smooth. But you never know."

I wanted to be there when the well came in, but who knew when that would be. I told Clarence we better head back.

"You cross your fingers," I told Tye, and then thanked his crew for their hard work. We rode back to the ranch, getting home in midafternoon.

Weldon Stanley was waiting for us at the pens. Standing by a jaded horse, he looked upset.

"You look like there's something terrible wrong."

"Turk and I spotted three guys slow-elking one of our fat cows."

"Where's Turk?"

"He's on foot and all right, but they shot his horse out from under him. He's got a rifle and told me to ride like hell and get help. I just got here."

"Clarence, get us some horses ready. I'll get some more ammo just in case." I was backpedaling for my office while talking to them. "That's up on Buckskin flats?"

Weldon said, "That's where we found them butchering it."

Norman and his helper came on the run. "What's wrong?"

"Rustlers. They shot Turk's horse. Weldon said he was fine and came back for help and a horse for him."

"You want me to send the crew up there when they come in?"

"Yes. Stick some food in their hands. We may be out all night looking for them."

"We can do that."

"Buckskin Flats is where they need to start. They can trail us from there."

"What if the old man asks what's the ruckus?" Norman asked.

"Tell him we're settling things. I'll be back to explain what we did about it."

Weldon had a horse on a lead for Turk. Clarence and I were swapping saddles to fresh horses. The cook's helper brought us some food and put it in our saddlebags.

"Thanks. Thank Norman, too." I swung in the saddle at last.

"Be careful, Mr. Gil. We sure need you around here."

"I'll try. You guys hold the ranch together."

"Yes, sir, we will."

We charged off for the flats. I was grateful both Clarence and I had our chaps on. I didn't wear them every day, but pushing hard through the brush and cedar could get your legs beat up, and it ain't fun to pick a thousand barbed needles out of your legs from a cactus patch collision. We hustled to get up to the site. It wasn't long before our horses were sweating and breathing hard, darting in and out on cow paths, taking a shortcut to get there.

At last I spotted Turk waving his rifle for us to see him. We reined up and let our winded horses cool off.

"I was hurrying all I could," Weldon told his saddle partner.

"I know." Turk handed him his rifle to bail on and rode the fresh horse bareback to go back for his saddle. "I ain't seen hide nor hair of them since they rode off, Gil."

"I bet they lit a shuck, but we have some hours before dark. They won't get away."

We trotted the horses north up the wide basin called the Flats. I saw the downed horse and not far from there the buzzards were already feasting on a beef carcass, no doubt the rustlers' kill.

"They were pretty damn brave not driving that steer they shot up a canyon or out of sight to butcher him," Weldon said.

"Or desperate. Most crooks are not that smart." I dismounted to check their tracks. Some boots make different prints on the ground.

"You boys know them?"

"I thought one was the Masters boy," Turk said. "He runs with some toughs anymore."

"It might have been him," Weldon said.

"Well, we'll be certain when we catch them we have the right ones."

"You know," Clarence said, "We've had some losses where we thought a big cat got 'em. You reckon they're that big cat?"

"They could be." We had to dismount to help Turk get his saddle off the dead horse. In the end we had to use a lariat wrapped on Clarence's saddle horn to pull and turn the horse over to get to the saddle. Free at last, Turk cleaned it up and slung it on his new mount.

Clarence had their tracks that led northwest, and the four of us soon were in hot pursuit, busting the brush and greasewood to follow their trail. We crossed in a low gap and went off the Whitaker range of hills. Three hours later with the sun dying over our shoulder, we rode down Hanger's Trail toward a small community called Roseyville.

"Track's going to get harder to read," Clarence said over his shoulder.

"They may be in one of the saloons," I offered.

Everyone nodded. There were some jaded hitched horses in front of Lasiter's Last Chance Saloon. In a soft voice, I told Weldon and Turk to stay outside. The rustlers might recognize them.

I bellied up to the bar like I owned the place and ordered a beer. Several customers gave me nods, and then went back to their drinking and card playing.

In the mirror behind the bar, I saw a man's hand shift for his gun and spun on my heel. My right hand filled with my six-gun belching bullets into the chest of the big fellow before he could shoot at me. His gun went off into the floorboards, engulfing the room in smoke and putting the candle lamps out.

The bar girls screamed. Men fled the room front and back. Clarence busted in with his handgun ready.

"Where the hell did the rest of them go?" he asked.

"They must be getting away in the alley."

"You all right? You know them?"

"I'm fine. They know me. One tried to gun me down. I got

him. We have them cut off from their horses. They'll probably steal more to get out of town."

A lawman with his white shirttail flapping and a sawed-off shotgun in his hands came running pell-mell up the boardwalk and burst in the batwing doors. "What the hell is going on?"

"The one inside is dead. He drew on me. His cattle rustling associates ran off."

"Who in the hell are you?"

"Gil Slatter, foreman for the TXY. These three men slow-elked one of our steers this afternoon. My men caught them at it. They shot one of our horses and rode off. We've been tracking them for hours. Go in there and tell me who that shot one is. I want his accomplices. What's your name?"

"Albert O'Bryan. I'll see what I can do about that."

"Thanks, Albert." I told the other two to ride the streets and alleys. "See if we can unearth them. I'm going back inside and see what that marshal found out. They might back-shoot you, so be careful."

"We will."

Turk and Weldon rode off. Clarence met me in the batwing doors. "His name is Kiley Masters. He'll live they say. His old man owns that Sutton Ranch."

"He talking to the lawman?"

"Some. He's acting tough."

"I want the others' names."

We both went to where they had him spread out on top of two tables.

"Masters, who are the other two?" I demanded.

"Screw you."

"You want to live long enough to see this doctor they got coming, you better start talking."

"You can't—"

He shut up when I showed him my jackknife and opened it.

"All right, all right. Humphrey and Radisson."

"First names?"

"Matt and Corbett."

"You three owe me for a good horse you shot plus a steer you slow-elked."

"Try and collect it."

"Your father might pay it to save you from going to Yuma prison for five years. I'm going to see him in the morning. But you ever do this again I aim to hang you by the neck until you're dead. Don't you ever mess with my ranch, cowboys, or stock. Come on, Clarence. His gang is still in town."

When Clarence and I got out on the porch, over half a dozen of our employees had ridden up on sweaty horses in the night.

"Boys, the ringleader, Kiley Masters, is inside. He tried to gun me down, and I shot him. He'll probably live. Matt Humphrey and Corbett Radisson are loose on foot. Weldon and Turk are already looking for them. Spread out and find them. They can all rot in Yuma Prison for rustling and attempted murder.

"I'll stay here. Anyone gets them, bring them up here for the marshal. I don't care head or foot first. Don't take a chance on them shooting you, either. They ain't worth that."

"I'll go with them, Gil," Clarence said. "We'll get them rounded up before sunup."

I went back inside. Masters looked a lot paler, slumped across the two tables. He'd lost a lot of blood. No sign of the doctor they'd sent for.

"That doc ever coming?" he asked the marshal.

"He might be delivering a baby," Albert said. "He ain't worried about you none."

"Get me some whisky."

I frowned at him. I would not have pissed in his throat if he was dying of thirst. My men could have laid up there dead till we found them after he and his gang shot them. They missed and killed a good horse. Worthless outfits.

The bartender brought me and Albert some fresh coffee. One of the snotty barmaids stood by the bar, polished her nails, and scoffed at all of them. I was sure glad I had Kate for a wife instead of using some dove like that one for my own purposes. I was damn lucky she wanted me, and it worked out so well.

The doc and his medicine bag came through the door. "Who was shot?"

Albert jumped up. "Kiley Masters. He's over here on the tables."

"Who shot him?" Doc looked around the room.

"I did. He drew down on me," I said.

"Well." That was all he said and went with his scissors to cutting off Master's shirt to get at the wound.

Hearing what sounded like shots in the distance, I went out the batwing doors—half out on the porch—and listened. Nothing else going on but crickets and night bugs.

I almost bumped into a woman easing back inside.

"My name's Clare. I got a bed out back. Getting late. Half price for a toss in it?"

"No thanks."

"You look stiff. I could rub that out of you."

"No."

"Suit yourself. You about killed that rich bastard's spoiled son in there on the table. He may want your ass over shooting his baby boy."

"He can come try me any day he wants."

She smiled. "I bet he can. I would really bet that he can't beat you at the draw, either. I never saw anyone that fast in my life."

I went back over to see the doc's progress on the wound.

"Bullet's in his shoulder. Four inches down and three to the left and he'd been dead. He won't die unless an infection sets in."

I nodded and heard horses arriving out front. I crossed the room and was out on the porch in an instant.

"We've got 'em, Gil," Clarence said from horseback. "They wanted to fist fight. But they weren't prize fighters, and the boys didn't rough them up too bad, I hope."

Each outlaw was being hauled by the collar of his shirt or what was left of it by one of my men into the saloon. They were ordered to sit down in two chairs. Under the lamplight, they looked bruised up.

"Bartender, these men of mine can have two beers apiece on me. Miss Clare here will treat you boys for fifty cents if you all are needing some recreation. I'll pay for that."

"Thanks," she said, not sounding too grateful for my putting her to work, and took the first one of her clients by the gallouses out the back door to her crib.

Clarence laughed. "She thanked you, anyway."

I nodded, amused. "Ten minutes ago she was desperate. Now she has business, she's not ready for that much."

"I wouldn't be either for that many." Clarence laughed.

Doc got the bullet out of Masters, then packed the wound and bandaged him. Then his two fellow toughs packed him off to jail with the town marshal herding them.

"Albert," I said before they went out the batwing doors, "don't set any bail for ten days on those three. There may be more crimes they've committed and need to answer for."

"Good idea."

I turned back to my fresh coffee and laughed at the crew enjoying themselves drinking beer and waiting for their chance to entertain Clare or her them. Half past three, the last man who wanted to lay with her came in the saloon's back door, looking bedraggled.

"You the caboose, Jed?"

"Yes, sir."

"Go back and pay her this five dollars, and we can pack up and leave. I have my bar bill settled. Thanks, Tony," I said to the weary barman.

Moaning and groaning under the stars, the men mounted their horses, and we rode home. We arrived at the ranch in the middle of the morning.

"Put the horses up and get some sleep. I'll go tell the old man they're in jail. Be up in the morning for work. You done good, all of you."

I dropped out of the saddle at the hitch rack and found the old man in a robe, sitting in his Morris chair reading a book. He put a marker in the page, and set the book aside.

"How did it go?"

"We have the three rustlers that shot our horse and slaughtered our steer in jail. They'll stay there for ten days before they can be bailed out."

"You didn't lynch them?"

"Never had a chance. They were hiding over at Roseyville in a saloon. The marshal come after I shot that Masters boy, and the other two fled. That worthless piece of humanity will live. The boys arrived and found his two associates. They put up a fight, and the crew didn't waste much time whipping them. Marshal locked them up. After that I spent ten bucks of your money getting the boys some beer and entertainment for all the hard riding they did."

"I'll pay you for that."

"I expected you to. They're good help. Word gets out how we treat rustlers, we won't have much trouble, I bet you."

"The hell you say. Old Man Masters will come storming over here to get that boy out of jail."

"Don't let him bother you. We caught them red handed. After they done that, they need to learn something out of this deal."

Grimes agreed. "You spent ten bucks on them in a saloon over there. They must have had a good time."

"Two beers and all the trimmings."

"Were they good looking?"

"No, just one girl there, and she wasn't a stage actress."

"They didn't know the difference." He chuckled some more. "You're making a great foreman. Keep up the good work. Any more wells pop up?"

"Clarence said they had water enough for a windmill in the latest one."

"Can't all be gushers, can they?"

"No, sir. But we will better use our range with these wells and mills."

"I approve a hundred percent. We should have done it years ago, but that was your idea. Hell, I wish I could ride with you and see all your plans. But I can't. Keep working on them."

"Selling cull cows next."

"Good."

Mandy came into the room. "I's could have you some lunch."

"I'm too damn tired to eat anything, thanks. I need to go to sleep."

"Take care of youself. We needs you, Gil Slatter."

"We sure do. Go get him ten dollars. He's been treating the hands getting them rustlers."

She did and paid me. I thanked them, then all numb, I went off to my own room and slept till the next morning. Despite our sleep, we were all draggy in the mess hall for breakfast. We started our cow drive that day, bringing the culls first into the main ranch for road branding and shipment to market.

I had several offers came from my wires, but Lincoln and Coffee were the high bidders. Next, I had to get those cows up to the spur, loaded in cars and sent to Fort Worth. I can say that in a few sentences, but there was more than that to it. I wired them and told when I'd need cars on the siding. The next thing was to make it happen. Those cull cows could bring fifty dollars a head, less the railroad hauling bill and commission.

I thanked the buyers by wire and offered them several dates I could deliver them to that spur. Then I waited for their answer. A boy delivered it to the ranch. They took my first date, which put a hitch in me to hurry.

The big thing was the relief on our range to have them gone. No telling how many there'd be more than my original guess. We had hay and would have to feed them at the home ranch when we got them assembled there.

Mid-morning, I spotted a buckboard with a spanking team parked up at the house. I figured it was that boy's dad trying to talk Grimes out of making charges against his baby. Sumbitch. I guess I'd see how Grimes backed me. The Masters boy had intended to kill me, and I wouldn't forget that. He deserved all he had coming for what he'd done.

"Who's up at the house?" Clarence asked me when I joined him for lunch in the mess hall.

"Old Man Masters. I figure he's asking for Grimes not to charge his baby."

"Will he let him off?"

I blew on my hot coffee. "No telling." I studied the scantily dressed dancer painted on the calendar hanging on the wall. I had lots better than her at home. "He asked why I didn't lynch them."

Clarence nodded that he heard me.

"See the twenty-fourth date over there?"

"Yeah?"

"We have to have those cull cows at the switch by that day. They'll have the rail cars there for us to load."

"The men are bringing them in today and tomorrow. I'll hustle them."

"I need a real count so we'll know how many cars we need."

Norm, my cook, was standing at the door to the chow hall, looking after our departing company's dust leaving the ranch. "I think that old man left here mad."

All I said was, "Good."

Those two nodded in approval. "He needed kilt," Norm added. "Boys said he tried to gun you down."

"I sure have the witnesses then."

Norm frowned. "He'd shot you, we'd damn sure hung him over that."

"Amen," Clarence added.

"Better see how the wind blows. I'll need a close count on those numbers to wire tomorrow or the day after. I'm going up to the house and see him."

"We'll have that count by tomorrow night," Clarence promised.

Out of habit I reset my holster going out the open mess hall door. Sometimes the walk up to the white-framed house to talk to Grimes was a long ways, sometimes short. I lost track of checking it, my mind was so engrossed in what he might have promised Masters.

Grimes sat in his Morris chair and nodded at me.

"Well, he was here, all right. I knowed you seen his buckboard. Claims the boy had been drinking. Didn't think when he tried to shoot you. Said he was in a lot of pain. I told him he was damn lucky he was still alive and when he got out of Yuma maybe he'd drink less and do better than he did lately around here."

"You didn't cut the old man any slack?"

"Hell no. That spoiled baby tried to shoot you. He needs a lesson he'll never forget. I told him your effort to arrest them was the only thing that saved him from being lynched. And he tried to take your life in return."

I nodded. "I have the confirmation on the cattle sale. They need to be up at the spur by the twenty-fourth of the month."

"While the men gather them, they won't need you for that. Why don't you take a day or two off and go treat your bride?"

"I guess I could. Thanks. She'll enjoy that, I am certain. I'll have Clarence set up on what to do."

"Good. He seems to be doing a good job."

"He's a good man."

"Don't fret none about me backing out. I'm backing you on this Masters deal."

"Thanks. I knew the old man was pretty powerful and what he'd try."

"Listen, deep inside, that old rooster knows that boy done it all wrong. He just won't never admit it, even to himself."

"I heard you. I'll be back. We can get them up there in plenty of time."

"Gil, I won't worry a minute about that. Tell her I said hi."

"Oh, I will."

It was short walk back to the mess hall to tell Clarence my plans and what he must do about wiring the head count. All that in hand, I went and saddled the gray and then rode home.

Home was a word I hadn't used since I was boy. But her place and her person meant home to me. Even in the sundown when I rode up and could hear the clack of the windmill I knew I was there. A sanctuary I had not had in my life for close to two decades.

"Is anything wrong?" Kate asked, looking puzzled that I was there in mid-week.

"Yes, there is. Grimes told me to take some time off and hug my wife."

"Well bless his old pea-picking heart. Is he getting senile in his old age?"

I dismounted and began swinging her back and forth in my arms. "No, he's still sharp as a tack, but he must have always liked you. Like a daughter he never had."

"Of course, my father never shared that with me. I think

him and Grimes had a permanent war they enjoyed. You don't war with him much, do you?"

"No."

Cord came up to join us. "I'll put your horse up, Gil." He took the reins.

"Thanks. How are you and her making it?"

"Better ask her. She's my boss."

"He's doing very good work. He's mowed around all our buildings and killed two rattlers since he started."

"I told her no sense dodging them," Cord said. "If they don't have cover or trash to hide in, they won't stay long."

"Thanks. Good idea. Food suiting you?"

"Yes, sir. She's a whale of a cook too."

"Good. See you at breakfast. I'm going to be home for a few days."

"Sure and thanks. I really appreciate the chance to work here for both of you." He led the gelding off to the corral.

With a soft voice herding me to the house, Kate said, "I worried about having him here at first, but he is polite and a real worker. Daylight will tell you the story. He is neat."

She sliced me some of her ripe tomatoes in the house, and we talked about the cattle drive while I ate them. Catching the rustlers. Masters talking with Grimes. When it had cooled some from the day's heat, we went to bed and made love. Me and my several-sizes-smaller wife—I hoped she wasn't sick. I simply hated to broach the subject, but I appreciated it if she was doing that for me.

The next morning I saw Cord's efforts. The unused lumber was in a neat stack on sawhorses he made so no reptile could get under them for privacy. Every weed and grass stem was level with the ground around the corrals and sheds. The old wagon parts and iron-rimmed wheels from something were gone. He'd replaced two corral posts, and the corral gates all swung off the ground.

"You've done well. What will you do next?"

"There's two sheds full of junk. She said I could clean it out, but don't throw anything away until she saw it."

"Sounds fine. Keep up the work."

"Oh, I will."

Before lunch she made a trip up there to his site and agreed most needed pitched in the trash pile. They both came back to the house laughing.

"What's so funny?"

"My father brought home junk he thought he could fix and filled those sheds with it. It isn't any more than trash, and he never had time to fix anything when he was home. Cord and I were laughing about all the odd parts he had collected."

"I was thinking. Has this place ever been surveyed?"

She sort of frowned at me. "Yes, there are steel corners set. Why?"

"Lots of folks are fencing. Be nice to have any stock we have able to graze the entire place and not wander off."

"We'd need a lot of posts," Cord said, shaking his head.

"I don't figure we could fence it all in one sweep. But we need to think about it in stages." They both agreed with me. So much for fencing.

She and I planned to attend the dance. Cord said he'd enjoy going along if we didn't mind.

"You are part of our family," she said. That settled that.

I'd been home about a day and half, and my wife had not said one cuss word. World record. No, I didn't mind her cussing, but she didn't want to and she did that for me.

Her and I went swimming and didn't get back till long after sundown. She had left Cord food in case we didn't return. Riding home she was sure acting pleased.

"I am so glad you came home to spoil me. I did lots of day-dreaming in my life, but it never was as good as the reality of having you and me doing things like this."

"It isn't hard to read your mind about us. I'm so glad you talked me into this. I can't tell you enough how pleased I am by all you do. You've lost lots of weight, haven't you?"

"Yes I have, and I'm pleased that you noticed."

"And so far I have been home two days, and you have not cussed once. You're a very determined lady, Kate Slatter."

She rode in close and leaned over to kiss me. Neat wife.

CHAPTER 7

I warned Kate before I left early Monday morning that I might not be home for three weeks making the cattle drive. We had a heady night at the dance, and my student was getting real good at shuffling her feet. Monday morning, I was back at the ranch by the time the men were finishing breakfast. The cull cattle were in a trap and doing lots of upset bawling from being away from their own range and grouped with all these strangers, fighting for a position in this new society.

Clarence met me at the corral when I dismounted and I handed my reins to the wrangler.

"We brought in three hundred and ten cull cows. More than any of us thought. I sent the buyers a wire, and they sent back one. We're covered. The date to load is the same. I have the chuck wagon loaded. I mean Norman has it fixed. I sent Weldon up to rent us some pasture if needed along the way. I have a hay contractor to feed them up there for as much as four days if anything happens."

"You sound ready to go. When should we leave?"

"Tomorrow. I'd rather be there and wait instead of run the last fifty miles."

"Good job."

"How's Kate?"

"Doing damn well. That boy I hired is really straightening up things for her too. How do you buy fence posts?"

"Hire some Mexican to cut them for ten cents apiece."

I figured at ten feet apart that would be five hundred posts to a mile. That would cost about fifty dollars, making the total to surround the section about two hundred dollars.

"That don't sound so bad, two hundred bucks for the posts."

"Be a lot of money for me. Will it be all right to leave tomorrow, you think?"

"Oh, yes, let's start them up the trail. We'll need everyone for the first three days—two days, anyway. Once we get them trail broke and the infighting over among them, they'll drive easy, but we'll be worn out taking them fifteen miles the first day."

Clarence nodded and grinned. "That's why you're the boss."

He had that right. It was why I was the boss. Trail drives were no new experience for me. They got worse or better the first day on the trail. We'd see how this one went.

"I'll have everyone up and ready."

"Thanks, Clarence. You did good. You talk to Grimes?"

"Yeah, and he listened and asked me all about the bull moving and if I knew about it before you did it. I told him you saw lots we missed. He agreed."

"I'll check with him, but you did the right thing. I don't hide the mistakes from him."

"I thought he was lot more disagreeable a few years ago."

"Him and Thorpe I think had a planned war."

Clarence laughed. "You may be right."

I went to the house and found Grimes eating in the kitchen.

He looked up from slurping his cereal. "How is the wife?"

"Busy canning. Her watered garden is overflowing this year."

"I bet it is."

"She used to hand water it, so the new system really aids her. Clarence says you know all about the plans."

He nodded. "I was impressed. Thought he was just a blacksmith. He's more than that."

I agreed. "We leave in the morning. Our man is lining up the places we'll need to stop. Tomorrow will be a tough day, though."

"Not near as tough as Thorpe and I had with them damn longhorn deer we got out of the brush that first time we made a drive to Abilene."

I shook my head. "I worked on that same kind of deal. I rode three horses into the ground that first day south of San Antonio trying to get started."

He went back to slurping oatmeal off his spoon before he spoke again. "These old cows will be a whiz for you two," he said, whipping his spoon through the air.

I smiled and agreed. He had lots of faith in the two of us. Maybe his generosity letting me have that time off was simply to see Clarence in action. Good he knew the two of us better.

The boy from the driller camp brought us word that morning we had another gusher at the site we'd checked earlier. I turned back and stuck my head in the front door. "We have another artesian well up under the mountain."

"Yahoo. We may change to growing ducks."

"It sounds good. I'll ride up there and tell you more later."

"Thanks, Gil."

"Yes, sir."

I knew I wouldn't get back until after dark and told Norman about that before I left with the boy for the site. We rode hard to get up there. Water was running off the hillside and into what had been a dry wash.

Tye and his bunch were laughing.

I asked him what was so funny.

"We had this well casing all threaded to screw a cap on it, but can't because it is so damn powerful."

They were all wet in the excitement, and all of them must have had hell trying.

"Well, when you get it on, why not take a week off before you move to the next site? I won't be back, but report to Norman at the cook shack. We're taking a herd to the Sparkle Spur siding and shipping them. He can order anything you'll need. He'll have a ten-dollar bonus for each of you when you get down there, too. I sure appreciate all the work you guys get done up here."

"Hell, Gil, we're loving this job. Thanks for the bonus."

I told him it looked wonderful. That much water hadn't flowed down that dry wash in fifty years. And then I rode back to the ranch. Norm had supper, and I wrote a letter for him to show Grimes about paying the diggers and about how much was coming out. They'd have it capped by the time I got back and could dig a tank to store the water in. His leftovers were sure good. My belly button had been rubbing my spine. Norm finally went off to bed after agreeing to handle the deal.

We'd had a great deal finding those wells several miles apart that would sure help scatter the grazing of the cattle. We'd have some dry holes ahead of us, but that would be after our gushers, and we could stand it better.

I was up before dawn. Maybe not fully awake, but I stood in the chow line. I met Hap Simmons, the man Norm secured to cook for us. The first night's campsite was on Lucia Creek, and he was familiar with the route. He promised to have a good meal since he knew the first day would try us all, keeping the cattle in the herd and on the move.

My eyes felt like two hot sand holes already, and we had not even left the ranch for the fifteen-mile haul. After breakfast, the boys put a bell on the big blue roan-longhorn cross bull and opened the gates. The first cows followed him and the clanging marker up the road on the way to the spur siding a hundred miles farther north of that gate. In no time cows were stopping to fight for the leadership. Bullwhips popped, and the stragglers rejoined the herd, but by then there were more disputes and falling out among other cows. Lots of head butting and damn mad individuals thrown together for the drive.

I saw one cowboy standing in the stirrup, chasing a cow going back to hell and gone. It took a good cutting horse to dissuade her, but at last the cowboy and his head-ducking horse won the match. The cow ran back to the herd headed for the railroad spur.

All day long, various cows tried the herders. A few managed to escape but most fit right back in, and after noontime and a drink they peacefully grazed with their heads down.

One more bad day I planned on, then half the hands could go back and run the ranch. Day two did not disappoint me. We had the same ones wanting freedom or an old place to hide out in the brush. But by mid-morning they were headed for the old North Star in a jog and churning up dust with a minimum trying to leave or return. By the time we were at the day's grazing, they were moving more like an army than a rioting mob.

I was drinking coffee at the chuck wagon when the boys came in for lunch.

"You were right, boss man. They are settling down."

"You boys that are going back, thanks and head for the ranch after you eat. We sure thank you for all your help. We'll be home again in a few weeks. The crew can tell you how ugly all those ladies of the night are up there by then."

They all laughed. I shook lots of hands of the departing men and then sat on a folding canvas stool to eat my lunch. I wondered some about my wife and the boy. They must be getting lots done. That place would soon be too neat. After lunch, I took a siesta in the shade of the wagon on top of my bedroll.

When I woke, I talked to Hap Simmons about how things were going. He said, "Smooth. You've got bunch of hard riding men that know the eddie-cut to use around a chuck wagon. Plumb nice to work for you and them."

"At least we aren't going to Kansas this time. That would be more road work than I want," I said to him.

"Your road man, Weldon, does a good job, too, picking how we can avoid having trouble passing through lots of places. Damn barbwire is being strung up all over. No way. I'd say for anyone there is no way to take stock up that old Chisholm Trail anymore."

"Cattlemen may need to buy a corridor though this country so we can get to rail spurs," I said. Things just got more complicated by the season in the durn cattle business. Regulations, angry landowners, Indians up there wanting pasture rent. It went on and on. Hell, as a boy, I filled some gunny sacks with food and frying pans and headed out with crazy cattle.

I told Hap how some near bare-ass Indians stopped ole Charlie Hatfield and demanded a dozen head of cattle for going over their land north of the Red River Crossing.

"I remember him telling them Indians, 'You bare-belly bastards, you don't get out of my way and stand back, I'll shoot you, and I'll have you to eat for my supper. I just love eating Injuns. You ever eat any?'

"The chief in charge shook his head.

"'By Gawd, I could eat you without gravy.' Then he got out his pistol and went to shooting in the air. He was an old Ranger and still had two more loaded six-guns mounted in holsters on his saddle swells. We never saw them naked red men again."

Hap laughed. "Good thing they did run. That old man wasn't kidding."

"No he wasn't. Later on my own drives I never tried force

like that." I looked over the herd. "Cut them out some limbers. I'll have to destroy them in a few days anyways. No way they'll heal going north all the time."

"Boys said you hadn't been foreman here for long. They like and trust you. Nice deal treating them after you caught the rustlers."

"It wasn't nice. Those men came and helped me do an impossible thing. The ranch owed them for doing that."

"Grimes pay for it?"

"He did."

Hap shook his head. "Thorpe never got along with him, did he?"

"Those two were like two cats with their tails tied together and thrown over a clothesline. They fought to the death."

"I believe you're right. Everyone heard about all the shouting and cussing they did at each other."

"I get on fine with him. We're really getting the ranch in shape. Selling these old barren cows, riding better horses, drilling wells, making it a great working ranch."

"Lots of luck. You need my help, I'll sure try to fit you in."

"Thanks, Hap. You do a great job tending to these men."

Hap stood up to see better. "Something's wrong. Weldon's coming in hard."

The cowboy slid his lathered horse to a stop. He bounced out of the saddle and in his haste gave the reins to Paco, Hap's helper.

"Whew, Gil I run into some opposition today. Some guy named Waldorf says we can't drive those cattle on the road through his land without paying a toll."

"How much does he want?"

"Four bits a head plus riders and horses as well."

"You offer him anything?"

"No siree. I don't have any money or authority to do that. Said I'd take it back and tell you."

"He threaten you in any way?"

"Not really, except he did lots of cussing how he'd shoot all of us if we tried to cross his place. I guess that was a threat."

"Go find Clarence. We better go see this wild man tonight."

"Yes, sir."

"Where is Clarence?" I asked one of the men.

"Swimming in the deepest hole in this creek. That man is a river otter."

Laughing, Weldon remounted and rode south to find him.

I shouted after him, "I'll have fresh horses ready when you get back. Bring Bruce, too. He's tough enough to back us." The young man waved that he'd heard me and rode on.

"What's wrong?" the horse wrangler, Keeper, asked, looking half asleep.

"Weldon found some trouble ahead. Looks like we'll need four fresh horses."

He was off at a run. Hap found some twists of jerky for us to take along. It might take all night. While we were probably a day ahead in our plans and location, we still didn't need any detours or fees to pay.

Clarence, Weldon, Bruce, Gary, and I soon rode north to settle passage. If we paid one man, we'd have more that wanted paid. This was a road, not a driveway. It ran all the way to the Red River Ferry. We'd do something and get on with the drive. They could sue Grimes and his big lawyer in Fort Worth in a courtroom but not stop our good progress.

It took two hours of pushing our horses until we came in view of the new fancy-trimmed two-story house on the hill west of trail. We set our horses down. The big house had been recently built, but how three hundred cows going by would bother it I had no idea.

We spread out. The five of us started across the open ground side by side but at a distance apart and headed for his house. Someone came out on the porch, saw us, and went back to the door shouting, "Hell's a-comin'."

Next person I saw on the porch was strapping on a gun and holster set, tying the holster to his leg with a leather thong. He wore a real bright white shirt and looked like he'd dressed in a hurry.

"That's him," Weldon said.

"We get up closer, I'll have you all rein up, and I'll approach the porch."

The men down the line agreed with a nod.

At that point I had no idea about Waldorf's plans or mine, but we'd have this fee business straight before I left this place.

We were still a distance from the house when I told my men to stop. Then I punched the big horse in to go closer.

"My name is Gil Slatter. I'm foreman for the TXY Ranch at Dog Springs. I'm driving a small herd of cull cows to the railroad spur north of here. My man Weldon says you have a problem with that."

"This isn't a state or federal road. You're crossing my deeded land to get your cattle to market. I'm entitled to payment for that."

"Why don't you sue me?"

"What do you mean?"

"Get a lawyer and have a judge serve my boss and take us to court."

"That would cost money."

"It would be safer and lots smarter."

"I'm not afraid of you and your bums."

"Mr. Waldorf, have you ever been in a shootout in Texas?"

"I'm not afraid—"

"In every gunfight someone dies or is so shot up they can't walk or talk the rest of their lives. A rich man's son messed with my outfit and may die from the bullet wound. All his father's money may not save him. My men are driving that small herd through here in a row and if they crap on your lawn, I'll note it at the trial. But if you try to stop us, there will be bloodshed."

"You won't drive them through here."

"Mr. Waldorf, this fall there will be lots of cattle driven up this way. They won't come and negotiate with you. They may get so mad if you try to stop them they may lynch you. This has been an established cattle trail since cattle drives started."

"They won't cross my ranch."

"Do you have a family?"

"Yes, a wife, and two sons."

"I am not threatening you, but if you want to see those boys grow up, you better sit on your porch, and wave at them going by."

"You don't understand. This is my ranch."

"I understand you can go to hell screaming this is my land on your way to your own funeral." I waved off his protest. "Are you going to stop me or sue me?"

"This time I'll sue you—but don't come back and try to cross me again."

"Thank you, sir."

"Slatter, don't bring another herd down this way."

"See you in court."

"What's the deal?" Clarence asked when I gave a head toss the matter was settled.

"He's going to let us pass and sue us for trespassing."

"Hell." Clarence lowered his voice. "No Texas court will make us pay to use this road."

"He don't know that. You boys see any cow crap on his yard, let me know. I'll mention it in court."

We all chuckled and rode back to camp. I still had an itching about the deal, but the next day would tell. Some rich guy set himself up in ranching and didn't know beans about the damn business. Charging a cow passing fee was like pissing in the beans being cooked on the fire to most ranchers—a frightful event. But Waldorf would learn his lesson before it was all over.

The next day came. A little cloudy, so the boys around breakfast talked about taking a slicker along on their saddle. I tied mine on after breakfast. Weldon went up the road, and I told him not to get into any gun fighting. He agreed and another cowboy took the rag out silencing the bull's bell. Cattle went to bawling and in no time we were headed north in a long line. This day and one more we'd be at Sparkle Spur. Going too smooth too fast. I was on edge riding beside the herd but I had to keep an eye out for any sign or threat.

Damn cows bawled all day. I'd be glad to have that over with and be back home with Kate and Cord—especially her. I missed her words, her voice, and her presence. Funny how quick a guy could become addicted to having a wife. Sure fooled me. I knew some women early on in my life I thought I'd like to have married, but I didn't have a pot to piss in or throw it out. So I let that notion go by and rode on. Made some money on cattle drives and still had a good portion of it in a bank. But it never grew much in there and I wasn't convinced I could stretch it into a ranch.

Longer I waited, the higher the prices looked to me. Guessed I'd just go on being Grimes's step-and-fetch-it boy now I was foreman. I saw that big house and saluted it off my hat brim. Sue me you dumb bastard. Ha. Why, a Texas court would laugh him out of the courtroom, no problem. We'd be at Sparkle Spur in another day.

Lincoln and Coffee's man was there. Rod McKim rode out and met me. Told me the cows looked in good flesh and the cattle cars were coming. We put our stock in the fenced-in pasture that Weldon rented, and the hay man, Troy Conway, delivered us enough feed for three days, I thought. By the time that was gone, we'd have the cows loaded. I told the Troy to send his bill to the TXY Ranch at Dog Springs, Texas, and he'd get his money on receipt. He thanked me, and drove off with his two other empty hay wagons and drivers.

There were two good windmills in the pasture so the stock

had plenty of water. They filled up, laid down, and chewed their cuds. The drive was over, and all we had to do was load them. We only lost six in the drive. Most of those were probably escapees that returned to the ranch range. Three hundred and four head were going on the cattle cars. About fifteen hundred dollars less the freight, plus sales commission charges of four percent.

The horse deal was better, but we were rid of the dry cows, and that would save our range for producing momma cows. Our big sale should come in the fall when we sold the big steers that were two and three years old, plus the cull heifers in that class. I had figured we'd have fifteen hundred head to sell at eighty to ninety dollars per head. That should bring in close to a hundred and twenty five thousand dollars, and the ranch would show a good profit for my first year on the job.

I had to squeeze more money out of it. I was not sure how, but hiring outside help because some cowboy was too good to get off his horse and fix fence breaks was over. Coming up ahead, I'd take a hard look at the list of ranch employees and find if we needed all of them.

Maybe get Kate to look at it. She was good at figures and could settle it in a hurry. I needed some sleep, checked with the leisure crew around the chuck wagon.

"You men all right?" I asked the ones sitting around.

"Pretty well. We can use the rest time."

"Clarence find a water hole yet?"

A cowboy looked up from working on his boot soles. "Yeah, he's swimming over the hill."

"Hap, move breakfast back till eight in the morning. Let these worn-out cowboys sleep in."

"You have a deal."

"Good, you all sleep tight." I went to my bedroll and slept hard till sunrise. That cleared my head a lot. I joined Hap as the sun came up, and shortly he rang his triangle. An easy morning for the crew of men to lounge about and recover. Fix their saddles and tack. Catch up on letter writing. Hap had some paper and pencils for that, plus envelopes and stamps too.

Cowboy conversation like this followed: "How do you spell rat?"

"R-a-t."

"No. I mean like rat now."

"Oh, that's different."

Another hand piped in, "R-i-g-h-t."

"No wonder I couldn't spell it. Thanks."

Good guys, they ran from Zeke, who was the asking voice on spelling, to Hummel who spouted Shakespeare, and I damn sure could not understand his English. Or Fred who said his eyes were bad, and he couldn't see well enough to read. We all knew he couldn't read, and it wasn't his eyes. He had never learned how, but he could imitate any bird out there in the Texas brush. Some of us had talents that the rest did not share.

But these guys all could ride horses, rope, and made real hands day in day out. Like most good cowboys, they rode for the brand. I knew from experience that regardless of the situation, they came and in force. Like finding those two run-off rustlers in the dark of night at Roseyville. Or they'd still been looking for them. The low number of losses of turn-back cows was due to the men that rode for me.

Each man took a lost cow as an affront to his ability to sit a horse and hold up his part of the bargain. Made mine and Clarence's job a damn sight easier, and in the end, the ranch would be a better place because of them.

Keeper saddled me a bay horse after breakfast, and I rode in to look over the loading situation. I wanted to be damn certain it was secure.

Rod McKim must have saw me coming. He came walking over from the store-saloon and joined me.

That business was all that was there, besides the loading

pens. I didn't know Rod or where he came from except he was the agent. A shorter man in his thirties, I guessed, looking like ten thousand other Texas cowboys. A little bow-legged, he chewed tobacco and spat often. He shaved when there was a razor I expect and had a short laugh. His hair was trimmed, and he wore a nice 10X beaver gray hat.

He spat sideways. "You wanting to look over things?"

"Yes. You been here long?"

"A day. I wanted to be sure about them, too. They look sound enough."

I studied the rusty tin on the store porch. "Guess a man could get a beer over there. Any women?"

"A few. They ain't bluebonnets."

"I usually treat my men if they want some, and buy them a few beers after we load them."

"Damn nice of you."

"No. Men that work hard need some relief. We had a good drive up here. Lost only a few head. They deserve it, and my boss will repay me."

"You're new?"

"I was the under man before Thorpe had a heart attack and died back a few months ago."

McKim nodded. "You like the job?"

"I was ready for it. Lots needs done on the ranch, but we're doing it. Well drilling, culling cows should have been done every year, shaping up the bulls, trading in some horses."

"You sound busy. You married?"

"Yes, I've done that since I got his job."

"Well good luck to you."

"You married?"

"Yeah, she hated me taking this job and being gone so much. But we eat better. Our place ain't big enough for me not to have some income."

"I savvy that. I'd like to have a place of my own, but it takes so damn much money to get it going." I took off my hat and dried my forehead with my handkerchief.

"Yeah, and money don't grow on mesquite branches, does it?"

I shook my head and put the hat back on. That was a God-for-sure comment he made.

"Maybe someday."

"She have any kids? I mean the woman you married?"

"No, she'd never been married before. She's a lot younger, but I don't notice it."

"Mine was a widow. She brought two. I had two by my first wife who died. So now we have six. That's a passel, but I love them all."

"I bet you needed a wife."

McKim nodded with a smile. "I had some hired help to care for the kids, but yes, I needed one."

"How's the cattle market looking for fall delivery?" I asked him.

"I'd say good. You have mostly cross cows?"

"Yes. I think this bunch has the last full longhorn cows in it. We use good British bulls." I could tell he wanted to steer clear away from straight longhorn beef.

"We'd sure like to bid on them. I'd get a little bonus if you do sell them through us."

"I'll keep you in mind."

"Thanks. Want a beer?"

"I really don't drink beer or whiskey, but I'd go along."

"They probably have coffee."

I met the bartender Jake, and he made me a cup. Rod sipped on a tall stein of beer, and we discussed things in our past. Driving herds to Kansas and even the war. Like me, he was proud Texas had Rangers again, and the carpetbaggers were finally gone from our state. It would be a few years before the new force of lawmen had enough experience to hold down the wild ones, but that too would come. At least those Buffalo soldiers that had enforced the occupier's law with their bayoneted rifles were all gone. Texas could move on.

But with my brothers dead, lots of families broken up, and Texas deep in debt, if it hadn't been for the Kansas railheads and the cattle sales up there, we would have been in a real sorry state when the feds left Austin.

After more talk about state politics and two cups of coffee, I shook McKim's hand and told him we'd be there to load in the morning.

"Those cars should be parked over there today. See you then. Thanks. I ever get down your way I'll drop by and see you."

"Anytime. Folks can direct you."

I left the small saloon-store and headed for camp. After the next day, we could head home. And I could go see my wife. That appealed to me most of all.

The next morning, we ate breakfast before dawn. Horses saddled up, when the first pink of dawn's light peeked over the horizon we headed for Sparkle. Bawling cows hit the road fine. Not as much bucking as I expected. Sometimes on drives like this, there were show-off cows that would buck and jump like little kids set free from church when they hit the trail again. They didn't do enough of that to stampede, though, so the job of penning them went well. Dust boiled up during the sorting into carload groups. Some of the men were on foot working the gates, while others on our good cutting horses separated them for the next car.

The little donkey steam engine moved the next two cars in place to load, and the toot of the engineer's air horn upset the cattle.

"I wish to hell he had that damn horn up his ass," Clarence said, sitting on the fence with Rod, both counting the loaded cattle to be sure the number was right.

I agreed but had no idea how to make him quit. Two cars loaded, the conductor waved him to back up.

Toot!

Enough of that. I rode my horse over by the man doing the waving. "Can you tell him to stop that damn whistle blowing? Every time he does that, it spooks the cattle, and they might flatten these pens."

"Sure." Then he hollered loud enough you could have heard him down at home. "Quit tooting your horn until we get loaded."

The engineer waved that he understood. Clarence and I nodded at each other. Rod spat and smiled. We had no more horn blowing, and in two hours had the cows loaded. Rod assured me the check would be cut in a week and mailed to us. I told him I'd keep him in mind for the fall delivery. He shook hands with all of us and the horn blower, and that crew left for Fort Worth with the cows. Then I had a talk with the crew.

"Now it's two o'clock. They have a free lunch counter setup over at the store. He promised me plenty of food. Clarence has tickets good for three beers and a pass for them in the back rooms. If you ain't in camp and ready to leave at dawn, find your own way home. Any questions?"

"Thanks, Gil, from all of us," Hummel the Shakespearean shouted and waved his hat in the air. "We shall be there as requested, my lord."

"I'm going to stay here just in case." Clarence grinned big at me.

I agreed and mounted up to ride back to our camp. I'd caught a glance or two at the doves that worked there and had no thoughts about attending them—besides, I was married to a helluva good woman and had no desires for anyone else.

Hap and I talked about good dogs we had in our lives that afternoon, and I took another siesta. Tomorrow would be another long day headed home. If I had not been the foreman, I'd already been headed back that way. Patience, I told myself and whiled away the afternoon.

Two days later, we crossed Elm Creek, and I told Clarence to take the crew home. I thanked the men and said I'd see them the day after at the ranch.

They cheered me on, and I rode hard for Kate's place. It was long after the cricket chorus started their night symphony I rode in the yard. I guess my huffing horse must have woke both her and the boy.

Cord came out in the starlight, wearing his boots and long tail nightshirt, no doubt made by my wife. "That you, Gil?"

"Yes, siree. How have you been?"

"Oh, fine. Here, I'll cool down that horse. I know she's coming, and she'll want all your attention. We've missed you."

I hugged his shoulder. "Thanks. I missed you as well."

"I wasn't going to cry—but you and her—you're like having real folks to me. I ain't never had any I can recall real good at it but I am. . . damn well beholding to both of you."

"No, Cord. I am sure she feels like I do. You are part of our family."

"Thanks." He sniffed and led the horse away in the starlight.

A powerful woman tackled me. "You did come home."

We kissed, then went arm in arm to the house. At the door, she peered off in the dark—I figured to look for Cord.

"He's fine. He said he'd cool out that poor horse I rode into the ground to get back here."

"Thanks for doing that. I missed you more than I thought I would."

"Everything going all right here?"

We sat down at the table with the lighted candle. Her nod was enough.

"Cows are sold. No injuries going or coming. It was a pretty uneventful trip."

"Good. I'll close the door. I want you in bed."

"Same here."

In no time, I was undressed and in the sheets. We held each other and kissed. I thanked the Lord one more time for finding her for me. She was a dream of a lady and I was grateful.

Next morning the three of us had a big conversation over breakfast about all that happened while I was gone. Cord shot a rabid skunk in the ranch yard. That was a worrisome item.

"I figured he was mad. It was daylight, and he was staggering around from pillar to post. Healthy skunks don't do that. I got her shotgun and killed him, then used a pitchfork to carry him up and burn him on a brush pile. He smelled worse burning that he did before."

"Keep your eyes out for any more."

"Oh, we will," she promised, then poured us all coffee. "We think we need some heifers to start a herd of cattle." She looked over at Cord, who nodded.

"I could look for some for you two. Then we'd need a saddle horse or two."

"Well, the team is rideable," she said.

"But you'd need a cow horse or two, huh?"

"That wouldn't be so bad, would it?" she asked.

"No, but you first need to register a brand."

"Oh, yes, we hadn't really talked a lot about that."

Cord quick-like agreed we'd need a brand.

"What brand will you use?"

"Will KT work?" Cord asked.

"If no one has it."

"Do you like that, or should we—" She stopped.

"I don't care. You two pick a brand and register it."

"Can we put your name on it, too?"

"Why not?"

"You don't sound in favor of us doing this."

"Kate, you two asked me. I am only trying to cover all there is to do."

"Good, if you're okay on this, we can start by registering the brand."

Cord nodded. "Thanks."

"Thank both of you for figuring it out." We all went to laughing.

"I need to get over to the big ranch. Check with the old man and be sure it is going right. You two need anything else?"

"I'll saddle your horse and leave you two alone. Gil, I'm proud to be a part of yours and hers lives. It's nice to have a roof over my head and folks that care about me."

"Keep killing them skunks and taking care of her. I noticed all the firewood you've split up."

"We've been canning, too."

"Good. If we go broke running cows, we can still eat."

We laughed, and Cord left to saddle the horse.

"I'm so glad you came home to see me. I told you before I missed you. But I'm glad you found Cord. He and I have hit it off. I'm sorry that I'm not pregnant. I don't know why I'm not."

I chuckled and hugged her. "We just will have to work harder at it."

"I try. Yes, thanks."

"Kate, I'm pleased as the devil to have you. That will come if God wants us to have kids. Till then, we have each other."

She smiled.

"And when you two are here working, I see you get things done."

"That we do, skunks and all."

The ride to the ranch was short. I arrived there by noon-time. The crew had not made it when I got there and dismounted. Grimes came to the doorway and nodded.

"You made it back in one piece."

I nodded. "The crew is coming. We had an uneventful trip, except some guy is going to sue you."

"Sue me? What for?"

"Trespassing on his place with your cattle. He wanted a fee to cross his land. On the cattle, then our horses and the men."

"What dumbass did that?"

"A guy named Waldorf south of the Sparkle Spur."

"He some kind of a fool?"

"He wanted money. I said I had none, so sue me. I meant you. He promised he would, and I said if any cows pooped in his yard, I'd note it at the trial. I am here to report no cows pooped in his yard."

"Crazy outfit. My lawyers in San Antone can handle him. Come in here, and tell me the whole story."

Seated in the living room, I gave him the story. When I finished, he asked, "He just build that house you are talking about?"

"I think so. We used the west road to go north to Fort Sill. I didn't see it last fall when we drove the cattle up there. It's a big fancy house."

"I can't believe the folks settling in this country. Why, he knows we all need access to get to the market or the train sidings."

"I guess he thought he'd make some easy money. I don't know the man, though I met him and suggested he try the trial way to collect his money."

"Anything else?"

"I treated the crew when we had them loaded. Cost you twelve dollars."

"Get him twelve dollars," he told his housekeeper. "I haven't heard anything from the drillers since they came back to work. He talked to me. He's excited about the gushers. His name is Tye right?"

"Yes. He's a serious worker."

"Anything else?"

"No, everyone worked. Norm reported to me every day. He's an interesting man. I'd never really known him. But you knew that already."

"He's the fussiest person I ever knew. Damn good cook, and he cares about the men, but he's no nonsense when it comes to the ranch."

"You sent him here when Olaf quit, didn't you?"

"Thorpe and I had some words about his cook. Olaf wasn't that good. I won that war."

Grimes merely nodded, and Mandy paid me the twelve dollars. "I's got lunch. You two come eat."

"All right, we will. My wife is coming home one of these days. I've grown used to this lull. She is near impossible at times."

"I can't help you." I shook my head.

"I know that, or I'd told you to do something about her." He laughed. "How's Kate?"

"Doing good. Canning lots, and they shot a rabid skunk while I was gone."

"They did?"

"I found an orphan boy needed work. He helps her. Does neat things. He saw and shot the skunk."

"Oh." Grimes stared hard at me. "I may need to go into San Antonio on business. Do you have a driver?"

"There is a young man named Weldon. He can drive you. When will you go?"

"I'll let you know."

Mandy put a plate of fried ham, yams, and green beans before me. Then delivered a bowl of noodle soup for Grimes. He nodded his approval.

When she was gone, Grimes blew on a spoon of his hot soup. "I wish I could eat that." He nodded at my plate.

"I'll enjoy it for you."

"Someday you'll be old. Thorpe escaped it, didn't he?"

"I guess he left you so that he didn't have to."

"Been like him. He and I came down here when the Comanche crawled all over this region. Lots of wild cattle were here, so we went to branding them. We ate beans and suffered all the hardships together. I was the one got the money from my mother's estate to buy this rough land. I offered him half ownership. He said he didn't need my damn charity."

"He flat turned you down?"

"Thorpe was hardheaded as any man alive then."

"He could have been your partner?"

"Should have been. His wife died when Kate was small. I offered to raise her. He told me no and hired a woman to do it. That woman was colder than an icy lake. How that girl ever survived, I never was certain. But she wasn't my daughter. When you said you were marrying her, I thanked God at last she would be free."

"She is free. She never talks of the woman who cared for her."

"I wouldn't, either. She was very strict and must have been there until she died. Kate was fifteen by then, and she lived by herself over there after that."

"I see lots of things. She's happy and free now that she's mine."

"Oh, I saw that when she came over here with you that day. She smiled the whole time."

"I'm grateful to have her, sir."

"No more than I am. What comes next?"

"Send some men up there to build a tank with horses and slips."

"Good. What else?"

"Do a bull survey. Make sure they are all sound and get a few replacements."

"Serious business. You think we need many?"

"Not much for that, but we need a good inventory. We have the cows culled. This fall we'll cull more, but not that many. We need more water development, but we're finding it."

Grimes slurped some more soup and nodded. "We're moving along. Thanks, you're building a great ranch. I see it coming."

"I better check on some things. The rest of the men will be here tonight or tomorrow. Kate said to tell you hi."

"Kiss her for me. We can talk more later."

"I will. Mandy, good to see you and thanks for lunch."

I left the house and checked on Norm.

At the end, Norm asked me. "You think he's failing more?"

"Oh, he slips a little, but he was bright today. We had a long talk. His wife is coming out to the ranch."

"What for?"

"I don't know. But I bet we learn in a few weeks what she wants. It won't be because she likes summer in west Texas. She's up to something."

Norm agreed. I made plans to set up the crew who would build the new tank and went to my office to write some plans. I had learned several things I had never suspected about Kate's background. She'd only told me a part of the sad truth. No one ever kissed or hugged her. No one in her life ever listened to her.

But Adelaide Grimes was coming for a visit. He dreaded that. His third marriage to a much younger woman had shocked everyone on the ranch over a decade ago. Mandy sure feared her—she'd told me so.

Adelaide reportedly lived a very busy social life in Fort Worth. I'd only spoken with her that day at the ranch when she asked me if I ever came to Fort Worth. How I could stay at the Grimes's town house. I thanked her and went on. Even single at the time, I had no use for her or any intention to stay at her house.

I could only wonder why she was coming out to the ranch in the summer heat. She hated the place. Or said so several times in his company and the rest of them.

I also wondered why in the hell Grimes had to go to San Antonio. I figured I needed to line up Weldon on the special food needs of the old man and any care he needed to do. The perils of him traveling there on a three-day or longer buckboard ride might kill him.

What would he be doing there? I'd probably never know

why. At dark I turned in, and the crew still was not back. They were coming slow, and I had no idea what was going on. Clarence could explain tomorrow. I went to bed inside, wondering why I didn't sleep outside instead of in the stuffy room.

But that was too much to puzzle through. I pumped up my pillow and then dropped my head on the goose feather-filled casing, missing Kate.

CHAPTER 8

The crew rode in mid-morning. Grimes and I had discussed culling a few more horses that showed their age. Culling a horse is always a tough business, but turning an old one that shows signs of being crippled out on the range is no big favor to him, either. He'll have to walk miles from feed to water, then eventually die.

"Well, they made it," Curly, the new kid, said, pitching hay off a wagon to the corralled horse stock. "Damn sure took them long enough."

"You looking for a new position as trail boss?" I asked the cocky youth.

"No, sir, but—"

"I say we listen to what held them up."

"Yes, sir."

To be an instant critic is easy, but finding the real cause takes time. The boy would learn that. He was trying to make points with me. But in time he'd grow up. At least he worked as hard as his mouth.

Clarence rode over to meet me. "The wagon broke down. Took a day to repair it. Really to patch it up. We'll have to work on it before the fall roundup. How was your wife?"

"Happy to see me."

"I bet she was. If she was my wife, I'd been happy to see her, too. Anything wrong?"

"We have about five horses in the remuda we need to turn out or destroy. Two have serious ringbones in their front lower legs. That bay they call Star One's hind hoof was wrecked, and he won't ever be any value. The other two are bad wind-broke."

"Is there any killer market in town?"

"A Mexican might slaughter them."

I hadn't thought about *that.*

"I hate to take them out somewhere and simply shoot them, but I can if that's our job."

"Let me check on that. I have another problem I want to discuss. Adelaide is supposed to be coming out here in the next few weeks. She may be doing that to get the old man to increase her allowance. I hadn't thought of that. Hmm. That might be the reason, at that. Anyway, Grimes wants someone to drive him to San Antonio on business. That's a good three-day drive, and with him on a soup and oatmeal diet, it won't be easy. I thought I'd ask Weldon."

"He'd be a good man, but I could do it better. I wouldn't mind. He needs a good caretaker along. I'd do it."

"The way he acts, it isn't to see her. I wish he'd scrap this trip, but he won't when he makes his mind up. Maybe send the two of you along with him."

"Sure, we could camp and stay over on the way if he doesn't feel like traveling."

"I like that idea. Talk to Weldon and set it up. One of you can ride a horse in case something happens and you need help."

"That's a good idea."

"Better than my first one. I don't want him dying on our watch."

"What in the hell does he expect to do over there?"

"He never said, and I never asked. Saddle up a fresh horse. Let's go see how Tye is doing at his new site."

"Coming right up."

I rode over and told Norm he was in charge. We were going to the new drill site in Boxer Canyon and probably wouldn't be back till late. He smiled and waved me on. Turning the horse around, I studied the ranch house. Why was he so set on going to the Alamo? No way to know unless he told me.

The drilling crew was thumping away. Even before we could see their setup, I heard the squeak of the cable and the putt-putt sound of the small steam engine, then another thud deep in the ground. Boring a well was boring to me, but those guys got their thrill out of finding water. I needed to be grateful they liked that simple deal. I'd quit long before water showed up.

Tye put his man on the cable and came to greet us. "How was the cattle drive?"

"We made it work. No real problems. How is drilling going?"

"We're down seventy-five feet. No moisture yet. I'd hoped to find an underground stream under the overburden crust, but no luck so far."

"I guess you have all you need up here?"

"We're fine. Had a nice break, and we're ready to punch in a new and better one."

"What if it's a dry hole?"

"I'll move across this dry wash and try the other side. I witched water here and over there. But I can't believe we haven't hit it yet."

"Clarence and I'll go back. You have a valve on that new one?"

"Yes, we finally got a cap on it."

"I'll build an earth tank for it."

"Sure, but it is a powerful force in that one."

Satisfied we were getting our money's worth, we headed back.

"I'm glad we're alone," Clarence said. "There is a red-headed widow woman up there at the dance I am kinda sweet on. What could I offer her?"

"You want that ring back?"

"No, she's got one. I never had a wife. What will she expect of me?"

"Most women I guess expect you to listen to them. Be loyal. Understand their problems. Be interested in their projects. Don't be mule-stubborn, and enjoy them."

"It's the enjoy them I like the most. But I ain't the foreman, and I can't take off like you can."

"We can fit it in if you want to a marry her."

"Thanks, I'll think on it some more."

"Any time. Just be ready for that trip."

"Lordy, I dread that. But I can handle it. Weldon will be a good man to have along, too."

Norm saved us food. He asked about the new well, and both of us laughed. "Dry hole so far."

"They must be easy to find. They're all over Texas."

Grimes made plans to go the next Tuesday that I passed on, and those two set in to load the buckboard. Things were in good shape, so I went home Friday evening for the weekend.

Kate was excited to see me and told me about her plans for the dance the next night. She had sewn Cord a new outfit to wear over there. She had it hanging on the wall. I approved of it with a kiss.

Then she showed me the KT Bar brand papers.

I nodded big after reading them. There was a six-week comment period before the mark was final, but she said they told her that was mere formalities.

So we were cattlemen and women, too. Now I had to find some heifers to start with.

Things were running smooth. The three of us went over to the dance. I let Cord ride my ranch horse, so he had some freedom. He looked sharp in his new outfit, and she'd already mailed off a cutoff of both his feet to Hyer Boot Company in Kansas to make him a pair of boots. That could take two months, but they would fit when he got them, or the company'd make him another. Most of us Texans found the Hyer boot shop going to Kansas, and it was the main one we used. Though boot makers were sprouting up all over, I felt I could count on Hyer.

My wife wasn't planning on spoiling him, was she? Naw. He was her boy if we never had one. No matter, he was an appreciative kid and growing up fast.

It was hot in the old school house. Not much wind helping either. I thought about Adelaide and how long she'd cook over here before she lit a shuck and ran back to Fort Worth.

Kate and I swept around the floor to the music like old pros. I was building lots of friendships with other ranchers and their crewmembers. Clarence showed up and introduced Kate and me to Kelly Stipes. She was in her late twenties, I figured, and green-eyed with flaming red hair. I'd bet she had freckles on her butt like that old bar song. . .but ain't she purty. And I imagined she had a fiery temper to match her hair.

Kate invited them to breakfast in the morning, and they agreed to show up. The potluck supper was a vast spread, but moving down the line, I remembered dessert this time so I wouldn't be tempted with prunes again. It was after the meal I stepped outside to find a private place to pee.

I had just finished that business when a massive hand caught my shoulder and twisted me around. Quick like I ducked his haymaker and danced sideways. Who the hell was he, and what did he want besides beating the hell out of me?

His next blow struck my shoulder, and I delivered a one-two punch to his face. He backed up and roared, shaking his head like a half-stung bear, then charged me. My fist made a from-the-knee shot and connected with his jaw. Even in the starlight, I saw his eyes go blank and his knees buckle. My right hand hurt like hell as he folded onto the ground.

"Gil, you all right?" Cord called out.

"Yeah."

A crowd had gathered around. Out of breath, I worked that hand and arm. "Who is he?"

Clarence came right through the folks surrounding me and looked down. "You hurt?"

"No, but I could have been. Who does he work for?"

"He's a hired thug. Boots Harold. Let's end his miserable time on earth and hang him. He won't ever amount to anything good."

"Hold up. We can't hang him for starting a fight. Why's he here?"

Clarence was there and grabbed a fistful of his shirt and jerked him onto a sitting position. "Who in the hell hired you?"

"No one—" That bully never more than got that out and my man went to slapping the piss out of him. I mean, my under-foreman was furious.

"I'll tell you!"

Clarence had his fist drawn back ready to bust his nose all over his ugly face.

"Masters."

That name slapped me. He couldn't convince Grimes, so he hired a thug to do it. That was what had happened.

My man rose up, still ready to smash his victim, and stepped back from him when he was on his feet. Then Clarence spoke with authority, "Boots, if your ass is still in this county when the sun sets tomorrow, you will be asking to be put away. And I promise you that will happen. Am I clear?"

No answer.

Clarence swiftly kicked him in the leg. "Am I?"

"I won't be here."

"You better be gone. Now get the hell out of here. Folks came here to enjoy themselves without the likes of you."

Clarence stepped back, still looking seriously mad.

I came up beside him. "Guess he got your back up."

He nodded at me, watching the gorilla go off in the night. "The man hired him may be a rich bastard, but he's got an ass-whipping coming, too."

I never answered him. My mind was spinning. Masters was not taking his son's prison future lying down. By damn, I aimed to see he got all the law allowed. That old devil better hire tougher men than Boots to mess with the TXY bunch, was all I could think. My hand still stung when I joined Kate.

"What happened out there?"

"I'll tell you later. Let's dance."

"Sure." Then she grasped my hand. "You're bleeding."

"I'll be fine."

"All right. But you need to wrap it."

I dug out a handkerchief, and she tied it up, scowling at my wounds. "Who did this to you?"

"A big bull Masters hired to stop me from prosecuting his son."

"I'm sorry. It hurts me to see that you're injured. You're my husband, and I'll shoot him if he tries to hurt you anymore."

So I whispered in her ear, "He won't dare. He was exposed tonight. That boy is going to rot in Yuma."

"I still hate that he hurt you."

"I'm fine. Dance, dance."

"I will, I will. I only have one husband, and I love him." She shuffled with me to get back on the floor through the folks standing around the edges. Kate could really dance. She was a dream to wave away all my anger as the fiddlers sawed out a waltz. The night swept on.

We slept in each other's arms, and I savored the entire night of sleep. My safe harbor of peace and love.

CHAPTER 9

delaide had not shown up, and the old man was ready to go to San Antonio on Tuesday. Mandy fussed over him, giving my two men lots of advice on his care. Then she kissed him on the cheek, loaded him on the seat, and real stern-like said, "Don't you die on them going down dere, you hear me?"

"I hear you good, Mandy. I won't die."

"God be with you," she said, and they left.

I went about my day, figuring out what I wanted done next. I had four men using teams and drags to dig a tank to hold stock water. They needed a blasting monkey to go up there and blow up some large boulders they were working around.

Hummel was the man in the outfit who best understood explosives. I had three boxes of waxed blasting sticks, caps, and cords. They'd need to drill some holes with star drills in those big rocks to blow them up. So he'd need two helpers. I'd send them up there in the morning.

Turk dated a Mexican woman in Dog Springs. I'd have him ask around if someone could use the free horsemeat. That would be better than simply making buzzard bait out of them. It was such a tough job I hated to have to ask my men to do that. They would do it, but not without showing they'd rather not. Turk was the man to check on a use for them.

We used a lot of hay to keep the horses up close to our headquarters. I needed to look for some land in the ranch where we could grow our own hay, then find me a hay farmer. My cowboys didn't like that kind of work. But I'd figure that out.

I was shocked when I heard someone scream up at the house. I ran as fast as my boots would carry me to see what was wrong. There on the porch, screaming her lungs out was Adelaide Grimes. At the sight of me, she scrambled off the porch in a flash of white petticoats and a red dress made of velvet. The very ideal dress for the hundred-degree Texas weather. When she about reached me, she swooned and fell in my arms.

"My God, where is my husband? Has he died? He's not in the house. Oh, I know I should have come and checked on him. Where is that black wench that is supposed to care for him?"

In my arms, she weighed well over a hundred pounds, and her breasts were about to escape the low-cut dress. But that didn't worry me going across the porch with her to the couch. Laid prone on the leather, she sprung up. "Dear God, where is he?"

"He went on business. He left Tuesday for San Antonio when you didn't come."

"What for heaven's sake is he doing over there?"

"Ma'am, he didn't tell me. Only that he had business to take care of, so I sent my foreman and a very dependable man with him."

"You are the ranch superintendent. Your name is Gil." She used her palm to sweep her hair back from her face. "I am so glad that dear man is all right. I couldn't find anyone here."

"Mandy went to town for some supplies. She will be back this afternoon. Is there anything I could fetch for you?"

"Well. . . ." She shook her head like it was too much to tell me. "My clothing is way too hot for the temperature down here. Unfortunately, it all buttons up the back."

"That is unfortunate. Mandy should be back by four."

"Then I will bend my modesty and ask you to undo this dress."

She rose from the couch with no weakness apparent. Then she shifted her waist and posed her back toward me.

"You can wait for Mandy to come back."

"That is impossible. Unbutton my clothing this minute." Her shoulders shook under the dress as if she couldn't stand my denial.

"All right. But don't you ever ask me to do this again." My fingers fumbled with the many small buttons down her back. But the dress soon was shaken off her shoulders.

"Now lift my slip off over my head."

I did that, noticing how thin her bare shoulders were above the white corset.

"Wait. Undo the lacing before you leave me." She held it in place with her arm locked under her bust while I picked at the lacing, standing straight and tall.

I had no desire to see any more of her flesh and finished unlacing it so I could see the rounds of her bottom and her spine. I finished and headed for the door.

"Have you not seen a woman undressed before?"

I didn't turn. "Mrs. Grimes, I have seen several women undressed, but they were all professionals."

"Maybe you should think about turning around and looking at me. Some day in the near future you'll be working for me. And your job will depend on how you treat me, whether you have a job or not."

"I'll pass. Any time you threaten me when you're in charge you won't have to fire me. I'll quit."

"I own half this ranch now. You better listen to me."

"But he won't let you fire me."

"We may see about that."

I nodded, still not turning. "Yes, we may."

"You are a handsome man, Gil. I know you aren't that dumb."

"I guess you'll find out, Mrs. Grimes. Better pick up your clothes. Mandy may ask questions if she finds them there."

"Blast you."

I left out the front door and came off the porch. I had avoided her trap. She thought this old cowboy could not resist a near-naked woman. It was an opportunity for her to get a hold on me so she could use it to make me jump through her hoop. No way.

Norm was outside the mess hall, arms folded. "What were the hysterics?"

"She said she couldn't find her husband at home and thought he had died."

"Shame the rig brought her out here didn't wreck on the way."

I agreed. She didn't have freckles on her butt, for whatever that was worth. The future would be very tense having her there for however long she stayed. Damn, she was a real witch.

The dynamite crew went to stay for a few days to blow up the rocks in the site of the tank. That would speed them getting the tank done quick-like, so they could come back to ranch chow and their own beds. My visit with Turk made him believe that would be the outlet I needed for the stove-up horses.

I had avoided Adelaide, and hoped Mandy didn't quit before Grimes came back. If I was a female and had to work for her, I'd have already quit. But so far I had not done anything for or against her.

Adelaide stayed inside the house, no doubt because the summer heat was becoming oppressive. She'd already left for Fort Worth if he had been there. I suspected this visit was about her money situation. I heard Grimes had threatened to stop her spending money like it was water in the Gulf, or he would curtail it from her.

On Sunday morning, Mandy came down to the mess house and asked if I had anyone who would take Adelaide to church in Dog Springs. I said I would send someone with a buckboard, but we had to hitch a team and get the boy to drive her.

Mandy shook her head. "She would appreciate that." Then she shielded her mouth. "And I'd have a few hours of peace. Thank the Lord."

"Amen. I'll get one of the boys to take her."

"Good. I better get back. She'll need her hair fixed again."

"Mandy, you have my best wishes."

"No, I don't, or you'd killed her for me."

I told Norm's helper to find Earl. He was going to be her chauffeur for the drive. Earl showed up. Keeper had the team harnessed by then, and Earl was tucking in his shirttail.

"Drive safely. Don't do anything to her."

"Oh, I wouldn't do nothing."

"Earl, I don't care what happens, but don't even kiss her."

"Yes, sir. I mean—I won't."

"Drive easy."

"I will, I will."

"Good. She wants to go to church. Help her on and off the buckboard."

"Yes."

"Go pick her up." He left in a run for the buckboard.

Norm was in the door, suppressing his amusement overhearing me. "You think she'd treat him to her body going in there?"

"I don't know what she'd do. I don't need anything until after Grimes comes back home. She's his problem."

"I'm sorry. You're doing a good job to keep the peace until then. Better than I would."

The church trip was uneventful. Mandy had three hours of peace and quiet, and I felt like I'd survived another disaster.

Midday Wednesday, a very weary Grimes returned and had to be helped in the house by his two men. He was worn out, so they'd taken an extra day coming back so he could rest.

"Adelaide was cuddling him when we left."

"What did he do in San Antonio?"

"Spent four hours at his big attorney's office. Thurgood, Miles, and Bacon. That wore him down, but he kept saying, 'I managed to have that changed.' But he never said what that was. We didn't ask. He never was bossy or bad talking, and even apologized for his weak condition."

"I guess we won't ever know what he did down there, but it was damn important to him. He knew in his condition he was challenging death to get it done."

"Watch things, Clarence. I sent Hummel up to dynamite a big rock formation in the new tank. Turk thinks the Mexicans in town will take the stove-up horses. The rest is business as usual. I am going to get away from here for two days. Oh, Tye has not reported any water up there in the canyon site, and may move his rig if he doesn't hit some soon."

"Tell Kate hi for me."

"I will."

I saddled the gray and rode home, Arriving about midnight and waking Kate and Cord. We had a brief reunion. Damn, it was good to be home and with her as well. I hugged and kissed her.

"I know you're tired. Tell me all about it tomorrow."

We made love, and I even slept in the next morning.

After she cooked me a special breakfast, we sat around and talked.

"What is his wife like?"

"I never trusted her. She's a user. And it is all to her advantage. We think she came to the ranch in the summertime to get more money from him. The word is he told her she spent too much and to cut back. What he did in San Antonio is still a secret, but he spent several hours behind closed door with his lawyers, and came out and said he got it all changed. No one knows what that is. How much she will get this time is something we don't know."

"Oh, Gil, you have been under so much pressure I hope you can throw off the yoke."

"I will. One day with you is enough fresh air to make me recover. What's Cord doing?"

"I had a little money, so we hired two Mexican boys to cut us fence posts for a small pasture for those heifers you're looking for. Cord is using the buckboard to scatter them out."

I shut my eyes. "Good idea. You need money, I have some, too."

She rushed over and hugged me. "I was afraid you'd be mad about it."

"Mad at you two? Never. But hire a surveyor to make your fence lines on your land."

"Our land."

"Our land."

"How long can you stay?"

"Another day. I'll be back to go to the dance."

"Wonderful. I really look forward to that. I'm enjoying dancing, too."

"So am I, Kate."

"You heard any more about the Masters business? He may be out on bail by now. His father, I know, is campaigning to get him off, but I hope they hold his feet to the fire." She examined my hand. "How is it?"

"Almost healed."

"Can you and I go swimming?"

'We sure can. But we'd have to ride the gray double. He will be fine. Leave the boy a note. He can forgive us."

"Oh, he will. He is so happy planning the ranch."

"So are you." I swept her up in my arms. "So am I, for that matter."

CHAPTER 10

I went back to the ranch on Friday to check on things and to talk to Grimes. He was still awfully pale looking, but sitting up. He asked me how Kate was doing.

"She's fine. Her and Cord are doing some fencing. They want to start a herd. They have a brand registered—KT Bar."

"Sounds good. How is the tank coming? I heard that Hummel and them came back."

"Yes, he did. Clarence said they blew up the rocks holding things up. He thinks they have enough clay in the bottom to make it seal. But we will fill it slow to seal it."

"What else?"

"Where could I fence and raise some hay on this ranch?"

"Why not along the Calico Branch? The soil is deep and smooth there. Lots of brush and cedars to clear."

"I hadn't really thought about that location, but I'll check on it."

"There was less brush when we first came here years ago.

I had several sharecroppers came by and wanted that land to farm, but they wanted me to fence it. A post-and-wire fence cost a lot of money, and I figured in a few years they'd pull up stakes for a richer place and I'd have to farm it. Me and Thorpe were damn sure not farmers."

"Hay is a big expense. I might cut it out and produce ourselves."

"Do some planning. I'm not a stick in the mud kind of guy. You want your bonus paid in heifers this year?"

"Perhaps, and thanks for the offer. I still have to fence a place for them to take up with the ranch before I turn them out on the range."

"Good idea."

"Is your wife staying for the summer?"

He shook his head to dismiss any concern. "She expects more and more money each year. I've put her on a fixed amount, and she can cry and beg. That's all I'm paying her."

"Sorry I asked."

"No. I thought I had to have her when I married her ten years ago. But it was a case of an old man really lying to himself. Thorpe told me so, too. You know we always argued. If he was against it I was for it. But sad enough, he was right that time. But I can live with it."

"You must be feeling better."

"I am. I need another gusher or a real big horse trade to really perk me up."

"Don't we all. I'll go up there after fall roundup and get some more horses."

"You and Kate going dancing tomorrow night?"

"Yes. She dances good these days. I knew she would."

"Sounds like fun. Clarence told me about Masters hiring a gorilla to maul you that time."

"After Clarence beat the tar out of him, they say that he left the country."

"No matter. Masters was a damn fool for hiring him. But he'll learn like that boy did."

"I plan for them both to get a good lesson from it. I'm listening close for what the law will do to them."

In few more scorching hot days, Adelaide had a driver I selected take her to Dog Springs, and she went back by the mail carrier buckboard to Fort Worth. I never spoke to her again, and she avoided me on purpose, I am certain. Mandy was glad she was gone, too. Our operation went on.

During August, Grimes took a half-day every so often to show me how he kept the books and told me to hire someone or do it myself—his right hand was getting shaky. So I inherited a new job. I was also made a signer of ranch checks on the First Texas Bank in San Antonio and three others. Grimes and Thorpe had started with that First Bank and by this time did business with the original owner's sons and even grandsons. He held a sizeable deposit there as well as drawing interest.

We got a letter from his lawyers that Waldorf's suit had been set aside as frivolous in the Texas court. I told Clarence, and he laughed. But area ranchers had picked up our story, and I attended a meeting over in Cody City. The others asked me about the man who I said was new to the west Texas cattle business and maybe had learned a lesson.

Big Ike Calhoun stood up and said before fall we needed to be sure that corridor was open or make it open so the herds going to market at that spur could be driven across his ranch. Ike asked if I would go up there with some others.

"He's very hardheaded. Anyone live up there and know him?" I asked. No one raised his hand, so I started to sit down. "I'll go if you want me to."

"You know him on sight. We'll pick three more men to go with you and talk to him. If he wants to play a hard game, we can get him served papers by the sheriff in that county. Anyone know him?"

One man stood up. "I have a cousin up there. I can write him and save you a trip."

I didn't argue about that.

"His name is Tom Peters, and he's also a rancher. I think he could convince Waldorf to let us through and save you boys that ride."

"Arnold, you contact him and let us know while we still have time."

"When I know, I'll write all of you a post card. Leave me your address so I can do that."

We all agreed, and I rode home the next morning to tell Grimes what happened. He agreed that was the way to handle it and thanked me. I went home midafternoon on Friday, met my swell wife and Cord. Things were going so smooth, but I had no idea where the next dam would break.

"We only set posts in the morning," she said after she explained the surveyor had cost me twenty dollars, but she had a map coming. He also left them some good markers where the lines were located at around our section.

We drove to the dance, and Cord rode my horse. I'd buy us some horses at Fort Sill in the fall for our place. The dance was a festive occasion despite the August heat. Several men who heard I'd been at the meeting asked me about it. I told them all I knew.

Clarence and some of the hands had ridden over and left Norm to run things. No problems, though rain would help all of us. Sometimes in August, a hurricane in the Gulf would drown us out here in west Texas. I kept hoping one would show up.

Middle of the night, Cord woke us. Could he sleep in the tent? There was lots of rain coming, and about then I heard the growling distant thunder. He was right, and Kate told him to use the other cot.

"I hope it don't blow us away," she said, lying beside me all curled up.

"It's a tough tent."

She laughed. "It may need to be. I hope the hail isn't too big."

"Maybe we should go in the schoolhouse."

"If it's a big storm, it will blow it away, too."

"My, you are sure rough talking tonight."

"Gil Slatter, I am just being practical."

Cord and I laughed.

I kissed her and went back to sleep.

In a little bit, I woke up. The rain was coming down in buckets. She had a lantern lit and hanging above us. She was all dressed in her clothes. I felt sure she didn't want to be caught in her flowery nightgown if we lost our cover. The hail was pounding on our tent, and I wondered how long it would be before the tent was swept away. Over the storm's roar, I could hear people out there battling their way to reach the school building.

The intensity let up some, though it continued raining hard. I kissed Kate and went back to sleep. We had a good soaking rain falling—thank you, Lord.

CHAPTER 11

he storm didn't cool things off much. We had more humidity, but it sure settled the dust. The calendar in the mess hall turned over to September. Clarence and I were in the shop with the new man I hired, trying to repair a horse-drawn mowing machine we used to cut weeds and grass down around the ranch headquarters to limit the fire danger later.

Mandy came down there to the shop to get me. She was crying. "Gil, oh Gil, I think he be dying. He asked for you a short while ago. He don't have much longer."

Clarence said he'd wash up and join me. I agreed, and hugging her thin shoulders, I went with her to the house.

"He's probably having a little spell is all."

When we reached his bedside, he looked awful weak and made me bend over to hear him. "When I go—you don't let her or anyone run this place. You are in charge. You—you will see. Tell Kate I love her. . . ."

I was down on my knees checking his pulse. None. Mandy was really crying by then. Clarence burst in the room. "How is he?"

"Gone." I rose up.

"Did he say anything?"

"Yes. That I was in charge. Don't give her anything. You will learn why."

"That all?"

"No. He said to tell Kate he loved her."

"What in the hell does all that mean?"

"We may never know. He's gone now."

"What do we do next?"

I shook my head. "Too damn hot to do anything but bury him." Clarence agreed.

"I'll write his wife a letter, and she can come if she wants. But we'll hold his funeral tomorrow afternoon. Send Earl to get my wife and Cord over here. Mandy and I will stay with his body and take him to town."

"What about his old driver?"

"He's been laid up with arthritis since before he went to San Antonio. But we'll see if he can attend. He was powerful close to him."

"You coming back here?"

"Yes, after I make arrangements. Tell Kate. He said I was in charge and not to let anyone run over me."

"He meant his wife as well?"

"He specifically said her."

"No one has to tell me when she arrives she'll be on a tear. She was when she left, and she'll think after his death that this is her place and money."

"Clarence, she can have it when they read his will, but until then, she won't get a thing from me."

"You handle that part. We may both need new jobs when she gets through."

"I've looked for work before."

"So have I, but I'm kind of liking this one."

I turned to Mandy. "I'm taking him to Dog Springs. You want to change dresses and go along?"

"Yes, sah."

"Go change, then. Clarence is getting us a buckboard. We'll wrap him in some blankets and carry him to the undertaker to arrange it all."

"God bless you, Gil Slatter. You be doing right. He was a tough old man, but I loved him like a brother. He don' never called me nigger nor didn't forget to apologize to me after he had a bad fit."

"We'll miss him."

"We sure will."

I sat down at his desk and wrote Adelaide a letter to inform her that due to heat he had to be buried. I was there to answer any questions. I also wrote a letter to his lawyers in San Antonio that he was deceased and any further instruction they had for me to let me know. I promised to stay until it was settled regardless, as I had promised him.

Both letters sealed, I made ready to head to town to the post office. Waiting for Mandy to change, I stood in the front door looking out. There had to be a connection between Grimes and Kate. He was too concerned about her just to be a partner's daughter. Probably never know the truth, but I could wonder. No better than we got along, when Grimes's wife took over this ranch, I might have to find a new line of work. Damn shame, too. But I still had Kate and Cord. That boy looked likely to become the son we never had—time would tell.

The funeral attendance was enormous. Grimes was one of the first men along with Thorpe to settle that part of Texas. Everyone knew him. Thorpe had a crowd back at his funeral, but everyone knew Grimes and came to see him off. Kate sniffed some—he was like an uncle to her. Even a few tough cowboys got wet-eyed. The Methodist preacher was kind to him, telling the crowd when the church was being built, they ran out of money for the shingles. He said when he asked for help, Grimes hired and paid three Mexicans to make them on the site out of cedar blocks the congregation hauled in. He went on to say Grimes didn't want credit for doing it, and he even supplied half the blocks. "Folks, that was who he was. May he rest in peace."

Then he said the Lord's Prayer, and they laid the old man to rest.

After services, I drove back to the TXY Ranch with Kate in the buckboard. Earl had the second one, and he brought Mandy home. His old driver Moses was unable to attend, but he told us thanks for inviting him.

"What will we do now?" Kate asked.

"You and I can stay in the ranch house until she comes. You want to go home and check on things, you can any time. But I have no idea what our future holds here. She may run me off when she comes, but he told me to sit tight no matter what."

Kate looked at me and frowned. "What does that mean?"

"I think he may be going to continue to ration her money, and the lawyers will run his affairs. But Kate, you could guess better than I can. She'll be a hellcat on wheels when I tell her I will do nothing at least until his will is read."

"What does that mean?"

"I have no idea, except his last words. Don't do anything until I am told what to do. He never said what that was, except hold it together."

"Will you be made the ranch manager?"

"Honey, I may be fired when his wishes are read."

"Oh, Gil, I doubt that. He liked all the things you did so far."

"She *is* his wife. If there was not any will at all, she would inherit the ranch under Texas law. If he left other instructions and was of a sound mind and body, then they will overrule in that case."

"He never said anything about his will?"

"No. Not a word to Clarence or the young man that went down there with him."

"I'll remake the beds and get along with Mandy. We can share the house. She's an admirer of you. I'll go by and see about Cord, and we can wait for the lawyers' word."

"He said him and Thorpe were partners originally, and he got an inheritance and bought the ranch and offered him half of it."

"I heard portions of that, but not any details. They both came down here and went to catching cattle way before anyone thought them worth a dime. When the war ended, they drove one of the first herds to Abilene, sold them, and came home what they called nigger-rich. Dad used his share to buy our home place. Grimes bought more land from the state. Texas needed money so bad he made hellacious deals on his land-buying. Some said ten cents an acre. No one wanted it. Not out here. He found that out and really dug in. This ranch is a big place by land portions."

I had never before known all those details. "Your dad didn't want any more land than that section, huh?"

"No, he thought Grimes was greedy for land. But it was sweeping what he did, and all with proceeds from large cattle drives. He bought Texas cattle for five dollars down here and sold them for a hundred up there. But no one else had any money for years but him to buy cattle and more land."

"Well, Mrs. Slatter, we'll call this home until we get run off." I caught her in my arms coming off the buckboard and kissed her.

"I'll do all I can here."

"I know you will. You worried about our boy over there?"

"No, Cord has his feet on the ground. But I'll check on him and do the rest of my canning I need to do."

"I don't ever regret marrying you, Kate. You have been a great star in my sky. Thanks."

"You ain't alone, cowboy. I planned, I schemed, I did lots of things, but I guess being flat honest paid off."

"It did. I better go check on my drillers this afternoon. I'll be back by dark."

"Be careful."

"I will."

My horse tender came and got the buckboard team. "I'll put them up," he said. "Good day, Mrs—" He didn't know what to call her.

"My name is Kate, Keeper. That's good enough to call me."

"Yes, ma'am. I was just being proper."

"Kate's proper enough, thank you."

"Yes, ma'am. Gil, you want your horse?"

"Yes. I'm going up to the drillers' site and see how they're doing."

"I'll have him ready in a few minutes."

"No rush, Keeper." I went on inside the house with her, and sat down in his Morris chair. Grateful to have the funeral over, all I could do was worry about what the future held for the two of us.

Tye and his bunch were located north of the ranch house about four miles in the cedar-live oak country in the hills they called the Pony Mountains. They were small, steep hills, but had lots of grazing and not much dependable creek water. I wanted a chain of tanks coming off the upper end if he could find water.

He'd been witching for it, and felt he had some places he could find liquid under it. The man was respectable with a forked peach tree branch for finding water sources. I had no talent with one, but would not argue with his skills. Special people with that ability were rare, but Tye said he had it since he was a teenager, and that was why he became a driller. He simply couldn't afford the cost of the equipment and steam engine to run it.

Bobwhite quail populated the country and boomed off when I spooked them. It was a hot afternoon, and every once in a while a breeze struck me. But heat was part of Texas summertime, and I never worried much about it. The wagon tracks in the grass went through the tall cedars to an old homestead Grimes'd bought up. It had a small spring but hardly enough water for a ranch house, let alone livestock.

A rifle shot shattered the air, and Lex half reared, struck in the chest. I jerked my rifle out of the scabbard, and threw my boots in the air and was grateful we were only in a jog when the bullet struck him. I had time to clear the stirrups and hit the ground before he collapsed, and bolted for some cover under a cedar. Three more shots cut through the boughs over my head as I gathered myself up to try and see who shot at me.

"You get him, Russ?"

"Yee-ha! Shot him in the chest."

"No, you dummy, you shot his gawdamn horse."

Hunkered under the canopy of needles and limbs, I couldn't see either man. But they were both north of me. Lex was on his side out there on the dim road, fighting death. I had a hint it was Kiley Masters talking to that shot-bragging outfit.

What the hell was he doing up there, anyway? This was Grimes's deeded land. Up to no good, whatever it was. He must have gotten out on bond.

The third man chimed in about where I might be. I didn't recognize his voice, either. Lying in those sticky cedar needles and wondering how to save my life, I wanted a breath of wind to cool me off. None came.

They soon decided my position. I needed to move east some more and hope they rode off, but they were not likely to leave without killing me first to silence my quizzing about their purpose for being there. On my belly and elbows, I went two trees away from my first spot. Then I focused on a clearing. It was only a gap in the cedars, but it might give me a shot at anyone who rode through there. They were cautiously riding around at a distance when I saw the horse's head come in the frame I held the bead on.

Those were the longest damn seconds in my life. I had the sight on one man's chest and squeezed the trigger. Gun smoke boiled out of the muzzle. But he was hit and down, and I knew it. I immediately moved again, more south this time, listening to their cussing me. I had one of the three, but I wasn't out of any crises yet. They sounded determined to find me, with Masters giving orders for his man to get off the damn horse and locate where the hell I was.

All I needed in this hiding spot was a damn diamondback rattler sharing the shade. I vaguely had that in mind crawling around when I heard him buzz at a distance. I froze, trying to locate the source. Whew, he sounded big. Masters or one of his men was coming in my direction. I could hear the boughs scraping on his chaps. He was that close to me, and I still couldn't see any part of him.

How close was he to the snake? That reptile wasn't far from me, either, and the man might drive the serpent my way. Directly the man let out a scream and went to shooting—I guess at the snake. I had only the gun smoke in the dense boughs for direction. I shot the Winchester three times at the sound, and I heard the third round smack him.

He screamed. "Come save me, Kiley. I'm shot, and the biggest rattler I ever saw just struck me on the arm. Kiley, I'm going to die."

"Save yourself. You see where he shot from?"

"No—I'm dying. Do something."

I retreated farther south under more cedars. Then I heard a horse gallop off. That damn coward was leaving his buddy to die. Was it a trick for me to show myself?

The wounded, snake-struck man was moaning and crying. He'd shoot me if I showed myself. I needed to find one of their horses and see if they'd done anything to my drillers.

He chose his way to die. But even for a back shooter that was a tough way to end your life.

In a short while, I found one of their saddled horses and rode on to the old homestead. It was getting near sundown, and Tye and the men were sitting around drinking coffee. He rose up to greet me.

"You shooting deer back there?"

"No, three guys were shooting at me."

"What?"

"I got two, but the ringleader got away."

"Who was it?"

"You heard about the rustlers we caught?"

"Oh, yeah."

"Well, their leader, Masters, must've got out of jail on bond. There were three of them. They shot my gray horse out from under me. I got one with a rifle shot lying on my belly. Second one was coming through the brush, and I shot him. Then a big diamondback struck him, I guess. His partner rode off and left him to die. I left him, too, figuring he was snake bit and shot, so he wouldn't live anyway. Besides, he tried to kill me."

"Wow, you were close to getting killed."

"Yes. Too close. How is the drilling going up here?"

"Slow."

"Any sign of water?"

Tye shook his head. "What'll happen now Grimes is dead?"

"As long as I'm here, you all have work. I guess whoever is appointed the heir might change things."

"Who would that be?"

"His wife, Adelaide Grimes, far as I know."

Tye nodded. "She'll inherit it, huh?"

"He told me to do nothing until I was told so."

"You figured that out?"

"No, but we should hear about it shortly. I expect her any day."

What would Kate think? I'd promised her I'd be back by sundown.

"What can we do about those bushwhackers?"

"You have some lanterns. We can go get their bodies, and you can take them down to the ranch tomorrow. I promised my wife I'd be back, so after we find them, I'll ride on down there."

"We need our guns?"

"Better wear them. I think he's miles away, but you can't tell."

"What can you do about him?" Tye asked.

"I guess if the law can't contain him I'll have to see what I can do myself."

Tye nodded, sending two of his men to hitch their wagon. The rest carried lanterns in case they weren't through at sundown.

They found the first one I shot dead. One man stayed there with the corpse to wait for the two coming with the wagon. Tye and me worked our way in the direction of the second man. I'd warned him about the rattler, and we looked and listened.

The man was silent when we found him. No snake about. He had no pulse, so we hauled him by his arms out of the cedars and up to where the first one laid. Then Tye and I went and undid my saddle to recover it. We'd need everyone to turn the horse over, so Tye told me they would get it and bring it with them tomorrow, and to be careful going home.

Losing the great gray horse was a big blow to me. I didn't care about those two outlaws, and I damn sure planned to get Kiley Masters for shooting Lex. Tye and I shook hands, and I set out for home.

Under the starlight, I spotted two riders coming across the flats.

"That you, boss man?" Clarence shouted.

"Sure. What are you two doing? Snipe hunting?"

"No, we're looking for you," Weldon said. "Kate said you promised to be back by dark."

"Well my, my, I'm late."

"How's Tye and them drillers?" Clarence asked.

"They're babysitting two dead outlaws that jumped me up there in the brush."

"What?" Clarence leaned back in the saddle.

"Near as I can tell, Kiley Masters must have seen me coming. One of his men shot Lex out from under me, and I hit the ground scrambling and got in the cedars. I shot one of them when he stuck his head out. Then another came through the cedars for me, and I shot him, and a rattler bit him. Kiley rode away. Then I went up to Tye's camp. They thought I was shooting some deer."

"Damn, that was a great horse."

"A great one. They're bringing the dead pair down tomorrow."

"Where's Kiley?" Weldon asked.

"I imagine on the run."

"We going to saddle up and go find him?"

"I think we better use the legal way—first."

"Whatever you say."

"First thing I wanted to run him down, but Texas is a real state again, and we need for the laws to work. I'll go and talk to the sheriff this time. His old man won't get him out of this."

Kate came out of the house to hug me and thank both men.

"Were you in trouble up there?"

"I was ambushed."

"Gil?" Keeper said when he took the horse he hitched at the rack. "This isn't your horse or saddle."

"They shot Lex, and Tye is bringing my saddle. We'll talk about it in the morning. Thanks," I told him.

"Glad you're all right."

"I'm fine. Thanks Keeper. I hate losing him."

"Me, too." He went off in the cricket-chirping night with the horse, obviously hurt by our loss as much as I was.

"He took that hard," Kate said.

"Yes. He had been a great horse for many of us."

"I'm just so glad you're safe and in one piece. I have some food in the oven. I finally had to ask Clarence to look for you. That didn't make you mad, did it?"

I hugged and kissed her. "No, you were concerned. For a while up there I was concerned as you were—maybe more."

"Oh, Gil, I need you, but you know that." She bent over to get my meal out of the oven. "Someone is at the front door."

"I'll see." Norm was standing there. "Come in. What's wrong?"

"You all right? I just talked to Clarence. That bunch need stopped."

"I agree, but we have a sheriff, and I want him to enforce the law first."

"They turned Masters loose?"

"People are eligible for bail."

"He ain't."

"Come in. You've met Kate?"

"Yes." He removed his hat and smiled at her.

"Sit down, Norman. I understand you used to feed him when he came in late. I'm sorry if I'm taking your job."

"Go right ahead. It's nice to meet you."

"I have coffee I can heat."

"I'll be fine. I was concerned about his mixing it with Masters and none of us there to help him."

"He rode away. Left a man dying from a bullet wound and a rattlesnake bite."

"You know them?"

"Never saw any of the two before that incident. I only heard Masters, or he'd be dead, too."

Norman agreed. "I'm going leave you two." He started to rise up. "You don't know the ranch's future, do you?"

"No. I'm in charge by his orders until I have new ones."

"His wife should be here soon."

"Tomorrow. I'll look for her."

Norman nodded. "You have my sympathy."

"Thanks. I may need it."

"No, you can handle her."

"I hope I can."

"Oh, Gil, you will."

"Come back and stay longer," Kate said.

"Thank you, Miss Kate, I will. You're a delightful lady. Stay there and eat your supper. I can find my way out."

I saw he had embarrassed her, but I didn't say a word until I reached over and clamped her hand. "Don't be upset about praise. He meant that."

"I still feel like the little girl when I'm here."

"There's no reason to be like that. You are a fine respectable lady and my wife."

"I'll try to play the role better."

"Good." I laughed, and she joined me, shaking her head.

We went to bed, and I was glad she was there. Neat to have a wife like her. I thanked God a lot for sending her to me. Tomorrow would bring more challenges.

CHAPTER 12

Tye and another man arrived with the dead men and my saddle at nine that morning. Keeper put my rig on a Comanche horse, and I rode into Dog Springs to talk to Sheriff Bill Benton in his office. He didn't talk much, but he said he understood the problem.

"Earl Masters has lots of money and some high-priced lawyers working for him. I'm not fazed, but they do wield lots of pressure and threats in court."

"You're telling me after two attempts on my life they can't hold him?"

"I can only do what the judge tells me to do. I'd throw away the key on him."

"Where is the judge?"

"Over at Kentonville right now. He'll be here in two weeks for trials, but the lawyers have his case put off until fall in this court, and I say they'll put it further off then."

"I want him arrested on new charges. I'll swear them out."

"He'll have three witnesses swear he wasn't there that night."

"I'll swear out the warrant for his arrest."

"We'll serve the warrant and try to apprehend him. I'm trying to make law work here."

"I appreciate it."

Benton stood up and shook my hand. "Wonder why they were clear up there?"

"I thought they were sneaking around and got caught."

He nodded. "Thanks for bringing them in. After today, if we'd found their bodies, I would have had a hard time telling who they were."

I went by Squire's Store and bought some supplies off a list for the ranch and Tye's camp. Tye and his man, Nick, had a beer in the saloon, and we went back to the ranch. The big stout bay horse was good to ride, but not near as smooth as Lex. That was my loss. We were back after lunch time, and Kate fed us at the house.

Tye and his man went back to the rig, and I checked on my books in the small office.

Kate came to the doorway. "They have come."

"'They?'"

"Adelaide has three men in suits with her."

"Well, that sounds important."

Kate shook her head. "What will you do?"

"Handle her."

"Good luck," she whispered.

I was at the door when she reached the bottom of the stairs.

"Good day, Adelaide. Gentlemen."

"Get aside. What're you doing in my house?"

"Adelaide, I am the ranch superintendent by your husband's orders. I'm in charge of his ranch, his accounts, and the assets of this ranch."

"No, no. This is my attorney, Andrew Hanford. I am Grimes's only heir, and this is my place. Step aside."

"All of you stop. Until the law office of Thurgood, Miles, and Bacon in San Antonio tells me different, I'm in charge."

"This is my lawyer," she insisted. "I am the heir."

He stepped up and spoke loud, "Sir, you do not understand inheritance laws."

"My instructions was I was in charge until I heard from them. No one was allowed to withdraw money, sell assets, or do anything until his wishes are told."

"I have informed them. We are taking over the ranch, its assets, and bank account to protect her interests," Hanford said.

"I don't want to challenge your authority, sir. But I am in charge until they tell me I am no longer the superintendent."

"Sir, are you denying us possession?"

"If you call it that, yes."

"I'll get an injunction against you. We will prevail."

"I can save you a trip to town. The judge isn't there and won't be for a week."

"Then I will have the attorney general do it."

"I am sorry, but you are welcome to stay in the bunk house. Mrs. Grimes can use my old office for her facilities. Until I hear from Thurgood, Miles, and Bacon or you do, my wife and I will stay in the ranch house as we were directed."

"Where is the closest telegraph office?" her lawyer asked.

"I'm not certain. There is a telegraph in Dog Springs."

"This man is my accountant." Adelaide pointed at another man with her. "I demand to see the ranch books." She stomped her foot at the base of the stairs.

"Mrs. Grimes, I'm in charge of the entire ranch operation, and until I am so instructed by the law firm, I won't do anything in regards to your request."

"You can't do this to me!"

"I'm not doing anything but what I was instructed by your husband to do until this is settled."

She turned to her attorney. "Hanford, the local banker will allow you to withdraw those deposits."

"We will go there, then."

"Adelaide?"

"What?" she stormed back at me.

"The man in charge at the Dog Springs First Texas Bank is Joe Hamby. He is under the same orders as I am under regarding the ranch business."

"I will show him my authority," Hanford said.

"You are welcome to my facilities."

"Certainly not." She stood at the foot of the stairs, seething. "Have your bags packed. When I come back, I'll have this ranch, and you'll be immediately fired."

"Whatever you think, ma'am."

Her accountant, some assistant guy, and her lawyer climbed in their hired rigs with her and drove off in a cloud of Texas dust. They would only be better floured with it on their fine suits that already were dusty. Where would they stay in Dog Springs? No telling. Maybe Mrs. Body's boarding house.

Mandy came up to me. "How long she be gone?"

"Mandy, don't worry, you can come to our place if we all get fired," Kate said.

"My, my. I just don't know. That woman be a witch."

I agreed.

That evening a messenger brought me a letter from San Antonio. It was from Grimes's lawyers. The letter instructed for me and my wife, Kate, to be in their office the following Monday at 10 a.m. for the reading of Earl Coy Grimes's will. After I read the letter, I looked up at the messenger. "You have a message for Mrs. Grimes?"

"I do have in case she was here."

I shook my head. "She is staying in Dog Springs tonight. No doubt she'll be glad to hear of this too."

"Will you sign the receipt?"

"Certainly. Kate and I will be there."

"Thank you, sir."

No need to ask this young man what that meeting would contain. Our fate would be determined that morning. We'd need to leave for there on Friday. Be another nice trip for Kate and me to take. I liked San Antonio better than Fort Worth. Maybe the Spanish influence slowed things more, but their great music was everywhere.

Before we left for the reading, I spoke to Clarence and Norman in the mess hall. I filled them in on our plans.

"What will be his wishes?" Clarence asked.

"He didn't leave me so firmly in charge not to have some plans. What they are, he never said. But next Monday, we'll learn all about what he wants done."

"Can we count on a job?" Norman asked.

"I have no way to tell you. We'll learn that Monday, and you'll learn by telegram after that."

"I wish you luck," Clarence said. "This is the best ranch job I ever had, and I'd sure hate to lose it."

"Hey, the deal is cut. I'll do all I can for all of us. Her attorney said she was the heir, and well, she might be. If not, they'll fight for a better deal in court."

"So all this might not be over Monday?" Clarence asked.

"Right. Trials go on all the time over estates. His will should be well-written by those big lawyers, but if it don't suit her, she can sue the estate in court and test it."

"You drive careful. We want you back safe, win or lose."

"Now, I don't know what Masters will try next. Make everyone aware of his threat. I don't want any TXY worker hurt by him trying to get at me.

"We'll be on the watch and always send two when they go out," Clarence promised me.

"Good. Keeper is looking for the best team. I imagine the one you took Grimes to San Antonio with."

"They're good, tough horses."

"I should be back by Thursday."

"Take your time and enjoy it," Norman said and nodded. "If we lose, it'll be a shame. I've got some faith in him doing something good, though."

I shook my head. "The truth will be out there next Monday."

Kate and I left early Friday and made Kerrville the next day. On Sunday with church bells ringing, we reached San Antonio and stayed in a hotel on the Alamo Square. Bags in our room, our horses stabled, we went and found a cantina, and had some good wine and a three-course Mexican meal. After the food, we danced, and Kate beamed in her new dress as I swung her around the smooth floor to the fine music.

"This is almost like a second honeymoon," she said to me while we sat out a few.

"Yes, our second one. If we lose our job, we'll go buy some more horses, all right?"

"Oh yes. Maybe we won't have to shoot any more outlaws."

"I hope not."

"So do I. It's cooled, and some wind is stirring. We can go upstairs and make love."

I agreed, and we went to our room. How had I lived without a wife for so long? No way to explain how I missed so many years without such neat sessions with a mate. Thanks to her for wanting me—yes, Lord, thanks for Kate.

CHAPTER 13

reakfast on the patio in the cool morning, and I could look across at the weathered remains of the Alamo where a hundred and eighty brave men died for Texas freedom. Smiling at each other under the lacy shade of the mesquite trees, we ate the fine food.

"Any breakfast I don't cook tastes better," she said.

"Oh, yours is just as good."

"What are you thinking about?"

"How Grimes and your father went out there and faced down the Comanche. Fought lots of border bandits to build a ranch like they knew there would be a great need for Texas beef someday and rounded up all those mavericks and branded them. Then they read on a poster there were cattle buyers with cash at a little place called Abilene, Kansas, ready to buy those cattle and there were rail yards ready to load them. How they ever found their way up there. How some surveyors plowed an eighty-mile-long furrow with oxen that winter from the Arkansas River Crossing to Abilene, and piled sod to mark the way up there over the grass sea.

"As a young man I went there that summer, but never met those men. I never forgot the first drive, a long weary trip of rain, hail, floods, and tornadoes. But I partnered a drive we got financed, and after that we had a chuck wagon and were organized. My partner, Ken Sims, died in a Wichita saloon gunfight coming home. He'd been delayed a few days, repairing their chuck wagon to take it home. My chase to run down his killers took three months, and I left them both for the buzzards in a dry wash in the western Indian Territory. After that I had enough trailing cattle and ended up working for Grimes. But it was time to settle down, and besides I found you or you found me. Thank God."

We went by taxi to the law office and, when we arrived, two more conveyances were parked there. I paid the driver and led Kate to the great double door, then knocked, very pleased with her appearance in the blue dress and the nice hat made for her in town. I was sure she would measure up with any other woman at the reading.

Mr. Bacon introduced himself and apologized that his partners were working in court that day. He and his staff were ready to read the will. Mrs. Grimes and her lawyer were already in the room.

"Thanks," I told him, and Kate nodded. We sat on the right in a great wooden pew. Adelaide and her attorney were on the left of the aisle in another such pew. A young man introduced by Bacon as Hiram Coulter was to read the will.

He began, "In this county of Bexar in the state of Texas, I, Earl Coy Grimes, being of sound mind and body do hereby bequeath my ranch holdings, my several and all my bank accounts in various banks for the management and their control to be held by my heir and executors of this will and estate, Gilmore and Kate Slatter."

Adelaide fainted, and her lawyer struggled with her on the floor, calling for smelling salts. When they revived her and helped her back into her seat, she looked completely devastated.

"May I continue?" the young man asked.

The lawyer said yes.

"Gilmore Slatter will provide my wife Adelaide Grimes with a sum of four hundred dollars a month as long as he has enough annual profits from the ranch to pay this amount. In the case she chooses to sue this will and its contents, she loses and will forgo any future sum of money from my estate. Earl Coy Grimes."

"Are there any questions?" Bacon asked.

"I want a copy to study," Adelaide's lawyer said. "I cannot believe her husband was of sound mind and body and did this."

Bacon spoke up, "Two physicians of good respect here in San Antonio will be a witness to that if you sue the estate. I must also warn you that we served the Bank of Fort Worth, and the account she has there is considered his as well and will be transferred here."

"Oh, no." She fainted again and spilled on the marble floor.

"Smelling salts."

"If I owe you, simply mail me," I said to Bacon, ready to send the wire to Clarence and Norm.

"Before you leave, I must give you letters to the other banks here in San Antonio to transfer those accounts to your signatures."

I blinked at him. "Other banks?"

"He had money in four banks besides the one in Dog Springs. Her account in Fort Worth was at fifty thousand dollars when we closed and moved it here for you."

"Oh my God," Kate said.

"And she wanted more," I reminded her.

"Now she lost that too?"

Bacon nodded. "I must say, come in my office."

We exited the room and were swept in his spacious room. He made sure we were alone before he spoke.

"Mr. Grimes came to us for help two months ago. He said he had been reconsolidating his accounts and discovered his wife was moving his money slyly to hers. At that point, he stopped her ability to move any of it, but did nothing about her own account. We researched that it was really his, so when he died, he said we must close it by his order and move that money to one of your others."

"I see now. She had lots of money in her account when she came to the ranch to pressure him and finally caught him to ask him to let her take more and add to the one in Fort Worth, and he refused."

Kate shook her head in disbelief. "Yes. Now she's lost it all."

"We are grateful to you and him, too." I shook his hand. "Has a man named Waldorf came by to sue us?"

"Oh, he had no real case. We sent him packing."

"Good. I must go north in a few months and wondered."

"He can't sue and win any money."

"Thanks. Thank your associates for the thorough job. Kate and I want to retain you in the future."

"I'll send you a contract. Sign it if you have no questions and send it along with payment, and you'll be the on our list as special people. So nice to meet both of you."

We left Bacon. Adelaide and her lawyer had already gone. I hailed down a taxi, and he drove us back.

That evening we really celebrated, and were guided to a fancier place to eat and dance.

"To think we started on a horse-buying trip that made a thousand dollars and pleased him to death. I can't believe all the money he had," Kate said.

"That we so frugally watched our expenses so close."

"Yes, crazy," she agreed.

"Do you think your dad knew about his wealth?"

"I bet not."

"I'm going to build a new house at the ranch. So Clarence can marry his sweetheart and live in the old one."

She gave me a questioning look. "You think he will marry Kelly?"

I hugged her. "He sees what I have and is jealous."

Then she shook her head. "I know why. You want to do that so he'll stay. He and Norman think like you do. I have learned that since I moved over there."

"Darling, that ranch will be the best in west Texas."

She nodded like she knew and took another sip of the expensive wine in her crystal glass. "Now tell me what else you dream about."

"Over in southeast Kansas there are some great bluestem grass-covered hills. I saw some of that country on a few side trips. That isn't plow land. That's cattle ranch land."

She shook her head. "The king is dead. His heir is ready to expand the kingdom."

We both laughed.

But she was right—one hundred percent.

CHAPTER 13

There were house plans all over the kitchen table. The contractor from Fort Worth was Kent Scopes, a handsome man about my age with a few gray hairs in his sideburns. Building large ranch houses was his business, and we had seen four he built. Kate liked them. Cord said they were castles when he saw the drawings and laughed how she and Mandy could never keep it all dusted.

His words drew a scowl from his stepmother. I saw it and about laughed, but held it in. In the end we settled on a smaller one, but not a simple bungalow. He also put in the plans to add two bedrooms on Clarence's house to be.

I was ready to take the fall roundup cattle to Sparkle Spur. Somehow being the head dog had put more pressure on me that I never felt running the ranch. I attended a meeting of the area ranchers. None of us needed to get our herds mixed in moving them. That would require many lost days to separate them. So individual lots were drawn. TXY was number three.

Number one said he would be on the trail by October first. Number two said he had less than two hundred head and would follow on the fourth of the month. I put mine down for the sixth, but said I might need three days due the size of the herd.

Someone asked how many I would sell.

"Eighteen hundred head."

"Hell, that's like a Kansas drive," one man said.

I nodded. "We have lots to sell this year."

Several laughed.

I wired my commission company, and they said they could get me top dollar for the cattle. It would take three days to get the cattle cars loaded and out of there.

I jammed the wire in my pocket and walked up on the porch. In a few weeks material for our new house would start arriving. It would require a trainload of wagons to get all of it out here. But I hoped the new house would reward my wife who felt bad she wasn't pregnant.

She came out in her apron. "You ready to eat supper?"

"Sure. The deal is set. All we have to do is gather them and get up there."

"Henny is going to watch Cord's operation over there. His two dozen heifers have enough to eat in his trap while he works the roundup. Thanks for buying them. He'll build a ranch for himself."

"He's working hard. I'll try to watch out for him on the trip north."

"He's growing up fast. I'm proud you found him."

"Oh, yes, and stop worrying about having kids."

"Oh, I simply have my down moments. I'm healthy, the doctor says, and you are, too, so one day it may work."

"I'm so pleased to have you. I don't want you to fret about a thing. We can go over to the dance again when I get back."

"That would be fun. Come in to eat, or Mandy will think we forgot her."

"I am." I guided her inside and waved at Mandy. "We're coming."

"Rounding up has you all involved. He was bad when he worried about it too much."

"Did he worry about it?" That struck me as strange, but everyone worried.

"Oh, yes," Mandy said.

"I guess when you're in charge, it rests on you."

"Sure enough."

"Mandy, did he ever talk to you about his wives?" Kate asked.

"His first one died before I ever came. Number two was a nice lady. But she died one day too. His last one only came by to get more money. He done fooled her, didn't he?"

I agreed, amused. She'd thought she was so in control. We hadn't heard any more about her threatening to sue us.

The next morning I went into town to look for some day riders, men who were willing to work a few days on our roundup. The regular hands were covered up cutting out the big steers and each day driving them in from the far off parts of the ranch. Section by section we were getting them brought in, feeding more hay that we bought. I needed to get busy on developing that farmland.

At the store, I talked to the Squire brothers, Carl and Mick, about helping us. They agreed to come tomorrow and make the trip. They had a neighbor, Tank Morton, and said he'd work.

"Bring him. We can use him. Know any more need work?"

They told me they'd look around. I shook their hands, and they smiled. I went across the street to Kelly's Saloon. I didn't come to town to drink before I owned the TXY, so I didn't need any and looked over his crowd.

"I'm looking for some day help. Anyone in here need some work? Step forward"

One drunk stood up. His knees buckled and everyone laughed.

"Hey," someone shouted, "you forget your man back here, Gil?"

I smiled at him. "I know I don't need him." They laughed some more.

With my respects to the barkeep, I went outside. There weren't any more horses hitched in town, so I started for home. Weather had cooled a lot. Evenings were cool enough to sleep. I wanted the drive over, the cattle sold, and the new house built, but I was always impatient with myself.

When I got up the next morning, there was a man standing at the hitch rail by a jaded horse under a big, bare horn Mexican saddle, busy rolling a cigarette in the predawn gray light.

"Can I help you?" I walked out on the porch.

"You Gil Slatter?"

"I use that name. What can I do for you?"

"A bird told me you need to find a clod named Kiley Masters."

"You know where he's crouched?"

The man lit the quirly, puffed on it, and nodded. I rested my back on the doorframe to hear his offer.

"I rode clear up here when I heard the word you really wanted him."

"I never caught your name."

"I never gave it. You want him or not?" He pinched the flat cigarette in his fingers and then drew on it again like it was precious. Next he blew the smoke out of his colorless lips, and licked them.

"I'd pay a hundred for him delivered to the county sheriff."

The man dropped his face as if in pain, and shook his head. "Damnit, Slatter, I ain't no damn dog catcher. I can bring you his scalp for a hundred gold."

"He's down in Mexico?"

"Hell, all of them felons facing prison time are down there or are in the Texas prisons."

"I'd like him there in prison and serving time for his crimes."

He started to turn to mount his horse.

"Hold up. Doesn't he have a gold eyetooth? I recall it from his smile."

My man smoothed his shaggy white mustache with the web of his hand. "Yeah. You want it?"

"That's all I can get—yes. My wife will be up and make us some breakfast. Stay for a meal."

"Kin I eat it out here on the steps?"

"I guess so, or come inside."

He shook his head. "I ain't fit to be in no decent woman's house. I'd eat it outside here on the steps."

"Sit down. I'll serve you out here."

"Fine." He looped a rein over the smooth hitch rail. Then he jerked up his pants and walked over in his worn-out boots.

"There still good mustangs left in the wilds of Mexico."

"How you know that?"

"You ain't got all them hobbles on your saddle I see for goats."

"I catch some good ones. All split mane like that one."

"I'd give thirty bucks a head for ten prime ones like him. Geldings."

"You might have to cut some of them. That's an interesting offer, if I say so myself."

"I can afford it."

He nodded his head. "I wouldn't have rode up here if I'd figured you were broke."

Kate cleared her throat, and I got up and took the plate from her. His utensils were on top of the scrambled eggs, fried potatoes, and ham with biscuits on top of that. He nodded when I gave him the food.

She was soon back with two coffees. Quietly she asked, "He need sugar?"

I shook my head and took the pair of steaming cups to set

down beside him. Then I retrieved my plate from her at the door, settled by him, and began to eat.

He paused to slurp some coffee and nodded. "You better keep her."

"I will."

"You're in the market for one gold tooth and ten of them mountain horses. What if I just extract it and don't kill him?"

"Suits me."

"I can do that."

"I can pay you for it."

"You're a trusting devil."

"I 'spect you will pull it or not make it to church the next Sunday."

He nodded. "Or I never will make it there again."

"I'm getting ready to make my fall drive."

"I noticed all them damn bawling lot out there."

"You ever met Grimes who use to own this place?"

"I did some work for him many years ago. There were some border bandits harassed all the folks up here. He wanted them gone and didn't care how. He paid me four hundred dollars, and they never returned. That was lots of money back then."

I agreed, then took out five twenty-dollar gold pieces. He put down his fork, weighed them in his palm, and slipped them in his shirt pocket.

"I ever need help again, how do I reach you?"

"Just buy an ad in the Montero's newspaper and say I buy gold teeth."

"I'll look for you to bring the horses."

He set the dishes down, hitched up his britches, and climbed on the gelding. Before he rode south, he said, "Thank that fine lady for such a great breakfast."

Then he rode away.

Clarence came across the yard with a frown. "Who in the hell was that?"

"Never gave me his name."

"Hmm?"

"I bought a gold tooth from him and ten good mountain horses he's bringing me."

"No name?" Clarence looked at me funny.

"No name."

"Who's gold tooth?"

"Kiley's. He's down in Mexico, no doubt living the life of a rich boy since he jumped bail."

Clarence nodded. "He won't bring him back alive for a reward?"

"Told me he wasn't a dog catcher."

"He wouldn't come in my house, either," Kate put in, standing by the doorway. "That tell you anything about him?"

"I'd come in to eat your breakfast," Clarence teased.

"Get in here."

"No, I already ate with Norman. But thanks. Some character, wasn't he?"

"Yeah, but if I had a fight, he'd be my choice to be on my side."

"Been a time but I'd like to have done that."

"After my partner got gunned down in Wichita, I lost the taste for it." And that was the real truth of the matter. "In the morning we go out the gate," I reminded him.

"Two weeks' drive and then we have five days or some more to come home."

"You want to go see Kelly today?" I asked him.

"Yeah. You be all right by yourself?" he asked.

"Go saddle a horse. Tell her we said hi."

"Yeah, she's getting anxious. I'll be back here by morning. I appreciate the chance to go."

"No. I appreciate you. Get the hell out of here."

Clarence waved to Kate and went for his mount.

"He may want his ring back," she said, rolling it on her finger.

"No, I'll get him a new one." Then I kissed her.

"That crew is really pounding nails already on my house."

"My wife is getting anxious."

"No, your wife wants you to be careful. She'll miss you. Look out for Cord, too."

"I will. Norman and the three men I'm leaving will keep this place held down."

"Oh. And I can still shoot."

"Damn right you can."

Hap was there lining up the chuck wagon. He had no complaints and really checked out the old ambulance. But he had to make it work. Keeper had sorted out a lot of good horses for the men to ride on the drive. He knew every horse in that remuda, his name and qualities, plus soundness. The young man was a walking dictionary about the ranch horses. No small task.

Curly Hanks had taken Clarence's place as smithy, and he could shoe one in a hurry. Most of them were barefooted, only ridden once a week, so they didn't need the expense of shoes in the Texas hill country. Tender footed ones worth anything wore shoes, but there were only a handful of them. I kinda looked forward to the Mexican mustangs the nameless man would bring us.

Maybe after we got back, Kate and I'd run up north and buy some more. Outside of the altercation with them outlaws, that had been a fine trip.

The day went smooth. The men's war bags and bedrolls loaded in the wagon, we were close to heading 'em up and moving north.

Kate and I shared breakfast early. It wasn't even dawn. Cord was down at the bunkhouse—one of the boys. Fifteen miles stamped in my brain. Weldon had been over the trail twice. He had hay contractors set up at two places where he was concerned the grass was too short. I couldn't think of a thing. All the stock had been road branded with a bar in full compliance.

Hap and the chuck wagon rolled north. The day's horses to ride pulled out of the remuda. Keeper and two boys drove the horse herd out the gate. Clarence went to put the bell on Blue, and my point riders knew their places. These steers would be lots easier than the cows. Not near the fighting among them we saw in the cull cow herd. Steers were much more matter-o-fact than female stock. And yearling heifers were the dumbest to drive I ever knew about.

Bullwhips cracked, and with lots of yelling and bawling, we went north. I didn't have much dread left in my guts like starting on the old Kansas drives. Things were pretty routine. There were some steers didn't want to go, and a few haints tried to break back, but they met fierce competition from my riders and soon went scurrying back in the line. In two days, boredom would set in on my riders.

That evening I found Hap's rig parked on a higher rise. He was seated in a canvas chair when I rode up and hitched my horse on the rope hitch line. He got up, filled a tin cup with fresh coffee for me, and we appraised things.

"What's it like not to have the old man chewing on your ass?" Hap asked.

"Not so good. Now I have to remember everything."

Hap laughed. "How did that old saying go? I wanted to be in Joe's boots, and now I got them on, they ain't as great as I thought they'd be?"

"That's it. You know in the end, I had lots of things he liked. My bull program. My drillers finding water. Culling all those old cows. He wanted to hear about all that instead of ass chewing. Him and Thorpe were original partners. And I think they made war so they didn't get melancholia."

"You won him over, I guess. You have the ranch."

"He started with Thorpe and him being bachelors. They both got married, but Kate was the only child both of them had left. His wife was stealing money from his accounts, plus she never lived with him. In the end, he really gave it to the rightful heir of the ranch."

"I never knew that. I ain't nosy, but when you married her, she was on the hefty side, wasn't she?"

"I guess if you lived months at a time by yourself, you'd do something to just to do it. She ate."

"No one?"

"When I married her, she told me neither her mother who died young nor his caretaker ever hugged or kissed her."

"Wow. Wonder she didn't get tetched."

"She's fine now."

"Oh, a lovely lady. I'm jealous as hell you got her."

"But you were like me—you'd never thought to ask her out, had you?"

"You're right. Till you got her, I never saw her laugh or do anything."

"She dances damn good now."

"That's when I'm most jealous, seeing you and her whirling around on the dance floor." Hap shook his head like he was there watching us.

"You know what she told me going to our first dance together?"

"No, what was that?"

"I'd rather go bear hunting as do this."

"Why, I can't believe that."

"I got a real keeper."

"You damn sure do."

One rainy day slowed us, but we made our goal. The herd was at the spur on time, and cars were coming.

Sitting aboard his hipshot horse, Clarence rode by. "Well, what you think?"

"You ever shot any fish in a barrel?"

"I think it would be a lot like our cattle drive—damn easy." He reached over and shook my hand. "Thanks. You made it that way. What are you going to do next?"

"Kate and I are going to go look at the bluestem country in southeast Kansas."

"That might be fine country for a cowman."

"It just might be that. When are you two getting hitched?"

Clarence looked off at some floating clouds. "When I get my nerve up."

"I want you to go find a nice ring. I'm buying 'cause I have yours. We get home, you go buy it and ask her."

"Will I have to wear it in my nose?"

"I hope not. We need to let these men off to celebrate when we get them loaded in the cars."

"Ten buck advance?"

"Yes. Get me a head count."

"What about Cord?"

"He'll be eighteen this next spring and had more experiences in life than you or I've had. Pay him."

"Kate may eat our butts out."

I shook my head. "Naw, she's a realist."

"I hope so. My mom ever knew what I did on my first trip to Abilene, she'da washed my mouth out with lye soap and beat my butt like a rug cleaning."

We both laughed.

Five days later, I rode up to his old house and looked at the fresh lumber framework reaching the sky on the hill. There were ten new split mane mustangs in the trap west of the old house. Kate came on the run to tackle me. We kissed and hugged.

Out of breath, she tossed her hair back to look close at me still in my arms. "You look fine."

"Not near as good as you do."

"I have something for you." She reached in her apron pocket and produced a small jewelry box. I opened it. Inside was a large gold eyetooth. I nodded and pocketed it.

"You happy now?" she asked, looking a little peeved.

"Close. You ready to go Kansas?"

"I've been packed for a week."

"We can go in the morning?"

Her brown eyes brightened. "Let's go."

THE END

a

NOTE

from

DUSTY

Dear Reader,

   Gil and Kate went to Kansas to look for another ranch. There may be another book or two there. If you like the series' start, drop me an email at dustyrichards@cox.net. We'll see how the vote comes out. All comments are invited and I answer my email. If you don't get an answer I didn't get it.

God Bless you, your outfit, and America.

Dusty Richards

Dusty Richards grew up riding horses and watching his western heroes on the big screen. He even wrote book reports for his classmates, making up westerns since English teachers didn't read that kind of book. But his mother didn't want him to be a cowboy, so he went to college, then worked for Tyson Foods and auctioned cattle when he wasn't an anchor on television.

But his lifelong dream was to write the novels he loved. He sat on the stoop of Zane Grey's cabin and promised that he'd get published. And in 1992, his first book, *Noble's Way*, hit the shelves. Since then, he's had 149 more come out.

If he can steal some time, he also likes to fish for trout on the White River.

Facebook: westernauthordustyrichards
www.dustyrichards.com

DUSTY RICHARDS'
150TH WESTERN NOVEL

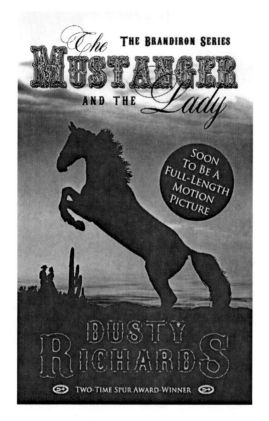

THE BRANDIRON SERIES

The MUSTANGER AND THE Lady

SOON TO BE A FULL-LENGTH MOTION PICTURE

DUSTY RICHARDS

TWO-TIME SPUR AWARD-WINNER

BOOK TWO OF
THE BRANDIRON SERIES

GALWAY PRESS

AN IMPRINT OF
OGHMA CREATIVE MEDIA

Western
Richards

1493792

CPSIA information can be obtained at www.ICGtesting.com
Printed in the USA
LVOW10s0230110816

499923LV00045B/649/P